Matthew Albrecht is a Texas native and resides in rural south Texas with his wife and two boys.

All those who lay captive to their captors. May you find HIM in the darkness.

– John 8:12

Matthew Albrecht

THE BROKEN UNDERNEATH

AUSTIN MACAULEY PUBLISHERS™

LONDON • CAMBRIDGE • NEW YORK • SHARJAH

Ordering Information
Quantity sales: Special discounts are available on quantity purchases by corporations, associations, and others. For details, contact the publisher at the address below.

Publisher's Cataloging-in-Publication data
Albrecht, Matthew
The Broken Underneath

ISBN 9781685629540 (Paperback)
ISBN 9781685629557 (ePub e-book)

Library of Congress Control Number: 2023903545

www.austinmacauley.com/us

First Published 2023
Austin Macauley Publishers LLC
40 Wall Street,33rd Floor, Suite 3302
New York, NY 10005
USA

mail-usa@austinmacauley.com
+1 (646) 5125767

I would like to acknowledge all the pastors in my life that have inspired me to see the light amongst all the darkness that our world can bring. I want to also acknowledge my wife Katherine who is my rock and inspiration that allowed me the time to write and work to publish this book while chasing our two young sons around our house at night.

Table of Contents

Chapter 1
Abaddon

My captive's lungs burned, and his soul felt tired as he took a deep drag of his Winston and flicked it out the truck window. He then proceeded to light another one. I could tell in recent years that his body had begun to rot and grow weary inside as well as out. Naturally, I can cause that in any one body that I make my temporary home. I am a natural drifter, you see. My basic mission at its primal core is to lay a path of destruction in any way possible for my overall time here is indeed limited.

I have been living in this present captive's body for over a decade now actually and have had much success in my efforts. The usual case being I only do reside in one individual's soul for a month or so time span. However, this captive was different. He was one that was capable of using his body as a machine to cause mass destruction. Therefore, instead of entirely consuming him, I would let his soul and mind come up for breath…but only every once in a while. For my captive is sheepish and unassuming with a forgetful face and no real presence to him at all. He is naturally silent and a blue-collar simpleton, if you will. What would you call it…white trash? The dark bags under his eyes lay heavy. His teeth are rotting from neglect, and for a man of thirty-four, he looks fifty-four. Life had been a hard road for my captive to say the least. By my natural presence existing in him, he too has grown to be quite a drifter. That is why he is my ideal form. My captive can blend into anywhere like the chameleon, not to be noticed to any great extent. That is when I can strike like a viper when the moment presents itself. Like it is before us this very evening.

We sat as one inside his rusted pickup truck alone in the dark, backed up into an alleyway up against an old abandoned building in downtown Gilbertson. Gilbertson is a sleepy and reserved town on the Texas gulf coast that blends in with all the rest that are scattered around it. For a population of forty-five thousand, it's really a small town that has some various big city amenities but no true ambition…or charm for that matter. I chose this very city for that. It simply blends in. There are dark forces at work here in this city. The Creator doesn't have that advanced of an army here, and I found it more than inviting to set roots here to cause as much damage as possible. The big city simply won't do. I have already played out my hand there and had just come from there, but only a few years back. Yes, as for the city, my Lordship is alive and well there. My fellow fallen soldiers have saturated that market. In any given heavy metropolitan area in the US, there are literally hundreds of us that have taken and invaded souls to do our master's work. It's little cities that are forgotten. They need just as much work, too, for our cause. It is there in those small towns and cities that The Creator truly has his pulse to build momentum. No, I wanted to come to Gilbertson to meet The Creator's force head-on. I wanted a challenge. It would later prove that a challenge is indeed what I got. Careful what you wish for, they say.

It is late May now, and the air is hot and muggy. Beads of sweat poured down my captive's face as he took in a large drag of his smoke and exhaled. My captive eyes were deadlocked on the prize before him: our prey. The marquee lights from the local dying downtown movie theater reflected its glow faintly across the truck dash and windshield. My captive could make out a scene as old as time being played out in front of us under these very lights. It was a group of high schoolers flirting to mate. The males were in hot pursuit to get the two females to submit as it appeared. Ah, young adolescents and their desire for the flesh. It truly was predictable. It was this desire that we fallen soldiers leaned on to then capitalize. For when you are caught up in nothing but the flesh, all else goes out the window, and you often then don't realize who is coming in. Me.

It was getting late now. The streets were empty, and any pedestrians or onlookers had gone home. This spot was a perfect hunting ground if needed to be called upon. The theater lay southwest of the rest of the city, which was downtown on the decay if you will. Besides some random law offices and struggling bank buildings, the theater was the only sign of life at night. So it had natural seclusion to it which is perfect when looking for your prey. My captive and I often would reside here some nights. Not much would come out of it, but tonight, I knew it was different. Our two male protagonists had been at it a while to get the two females into the car with them after what I presume was a social date at this venue. I was actually impressed by their effort. From one predator to another, I too know the discipline it takes to take your prey. It can take weeks or months of planning and stalking to do it right. You want to first choose your prey carefully. Then you must gather that information on your subject. You must learn their habits and their routines. That way, you know just when to strike at their most vulnerable moment. Tonight, however, was just luck. It was a trout line in the water that was caught. We were only simply at the right place at the right time.

The boys were not backing down, and after what seemed to be another twenty minutes or so of laughing, teasing, and flirting, we finally had a break in the monotony of their pursuit. One girl entered the car with the two males giving in, leaving behind our prey, one single female all to herself. My captive became aroused at the sight of the vehicle pulling away, leaving the young teen girl alone sitting on the curb. My captives' breath became heavy in excitement, and he put the truck in drive, keeping the headlights off. Roaming in the dark is where we do our best work; I'll have you know.

The girl stood on the curb, suddenly looking in our direction diagonally across the street. The gear shifting must have thrown her attention towards us. She stared at us for a long minute, making out what she could of our silhouetted truck sitting in the shadows. Only sounds were the night locusts now, our truck's engine rumbling gently in idle, and the subtle drone hum of the far-off distant interstate highway buzzing with activity. My captive's fresh cigarette glowed in the darkness as he took another puff to settle the nerves. We could then see that she turned quickly, walking down the sidewalk in the opposite direction, away from the truck and at an eager pace. Now it was time.

My captive slowly pressed on the gas and entered out onto the street coming out of the shadows now. My captive would gain another tonight to take home to feed me. My current captive and I, for years now, had preyed on the local young females around us in the greater area. However, we dare not take from where we call home, shall I say. We only took those locally if the opportunity arose that was just too good to pass. Case and point being now of course. Now, our efforts were indeed working, and we always worked to never lead a trail or take prey near where we dwelled in the city town of Gilbertson. My captive and I would ride all night at times hunting. We would go from county to county to find them and the perfect opportunity to take and then dispose of. Trying to find the ones that were alone, vulnerable, and or just asking to be taken. That was the challenge but also the thrill of it all. Sometimes it was luck, but most often, it was working to pursue long enough to get our prey alone in the prime spot.

In the twenty years that I had been living inside this particular captive's soul, we have taken over sixty-five females across the state. Numbers could be higher, but we are a cautious breed. From small towns to urban cities – it didn't matter if the opportunity presented itself. Younger, older, and of any race or origin we did take. However, I was prone to take the ones that were most loved by many. That way, I knew I was causing the most damage. To have that knowing ability was my…shall we say…not of this world six sense I was gifted and quite good at, might I add.

It wasn't the physical desires that drove me and my captive more than it was the aftermath. The wake. The cause and effect, if you will. That is what I feed on. The despair. The loss. The fact that we will kidnap and kill and that I alone will be the root of so many connected. Family members, friends, and community members will fall questioning their very own lives that will lead to a forest fire of doubt and rebellion. Rebellion against what or whom, may you ask? Faith? Exactly…and that is my mission. It is fear and total destruction. Turn as many away from the one you call The Creator and to turn them towards despair itself. Misery loves company, as they say, and where I am going, I want to take as many as I can with me.

As we pull the rusty relic out onto the street, we see our prey advance and break into a run. Oh, joyous. I can smell her fear all the way from inside the truck. This will turn into quite a delightful hunt after all this evening. My captive slams on the gas pedal, and we pursue and with any luck, we will capture her tonight. However, we will not dispose of this one so quickly. I am sensing this one's soul is less connected with others, and she challenges your Creator's very existence. Perfect. We will take her back to our dwelling, where she will become a fuel source for me. It will be ideal to have her at my disposal to take from her when I want, living off her fear and anger to then go out and pursue greater distances. This has always been the way.

Chapter 2
Cal Sullivan

I never thought I'd be the one to have a demon in me. I never really was picked for anything growing up...sports and whatnot. Rain hit our brown rusted out tin roof like nails this early morning. A crack of lightning had jolted me awake again. I must have drifted back off to sleep. Still, in my pjs, I rose from my bed covered in faded and stained Star Wars sheets that my momma got a few years back for my Christmas gift and went to my window seal. I pushed aside a few of my GI Joe's that clattered to the floor and sat on my ledge and looked out. It was coming down mean like out there. The open lot that sat directly next to our old faded white house was turning into a lake in front of my very eyes. School had been canceled for the day. Being ten years old, I considered it a downright holiday. Flash floods were supposed to be coming too today, so they said. The radio was squawking flash flood warnings early this morning when Momma was trying to get me up. It was 1987, and that weather channel was still fairly new. Momma said she liked listening to the radio better 'cause she never understood that radar screen they were showing. Only one allowed to watch TV in the house was Poppa anyhow.

The clock now next to my bed said 10:30. I knew Momma was up and had been up. The house smelled of bacon and cigarettes. The radio was still on in the kitchen, playing old country that she would sit and hum along to for hours by herself. I poked my head around my door and peered down the short hallway, looking across the haze in the air from my mom's smoke to see her there sitting in her moo nightgown at the kitchen table. I watched her as she wore a tired face of doubt while puffing away. She would watch the smoke dance in front of her face as it left her mouth. Momma, some days would never leave that there table. She would stay in her moo-moo all day, lost in

15

her thoughts, listening to the radio, going through a pack of cigs, and thinking where it all went wrong, I suppose.

My parents had been married for fifteen years now. I guess you could say five of those years were happy ? I had an older brother, but he had drowned in the creek outback beyond our house fishing one day. I was only two at the time, but I remember the day and the look on my momma's face. I remember it well, even at two. My brother and I shared a room then together. He was older by six years, and Poppa and Momma had gotten him a fishing pole for Christmas that year. He had the habit of escaping the house without Momma knowing and sneaking off through the back thicket of woods behind our house where the Cabeza Creek flowed. My brother that morning was up out of bed, lacing on his shoes while the early morning sun hit me in my eyes; rolling over to look at him. His gaze caught mine as I rubbed the sleep out of my eyes. With a mischievous grin, he put a finger to his mouth hinting to be quiet. Then just like that, he slid our bedroom window open, grabbed his pole, and was gone. I knew Momma would be mad, but I didn't have the heart to tell her and get my idol brother in trouble. I yawned and rolled over, falling back to sleep. I was quickly then awakened to my momma yelling and cursing. I sat up to see my momma running into the woods across the open lot that sat beside our house. A couple of cop cars with their lights swirling sat parked around the front and back of our house. Suddenly, a neatly combed hair deputy dipped his head into my room.

"You need to come with me, son," he said softly to me. He then reached down and picked me up with his huge bear-like arms and carried me outback behind the house to his patrol car. We sat there eating donuts together in silence. I saw more cops making their way into the woods now where my momma and brother had gone into that morning. In the silence, I could hear Momma through those woods too. She was wailing loudly, and I knew something had happened to my brother. I found out later he had drowned. Police listed it an accident and that he had tripped and fallen on a rock then rolled into the river and drowned while unconscious. Of Course, in small towns, rumors fly. Rumors said Poppa did it. He had been gone all that day on a job for work, but I couldn't believe that. I wouldn't.

From then on, my momma came out of those woods from out back of our house and never was the same way again. She was lost in a fog, and Poppa became quiet after that too. Been two years since he had stopped talking altogether, but maybe just to answer a question now and then. That is, if you wanted to risk the repercussions. He became almost robotic, never making eye contact. When he did look at you, there was nothing there. It was just a deep void that, when mad his eyes would flicker with an intent evil. Momma was unsettled by it, that is for sure. I didn't even like to speak to him. I kept my distance when I could.

We didn't have much money, and neither of my folk had much of an education. Momma never worked. She was just a zombie sitting at the damn table in the kitchen every day. I never really knew what my poppa did because it changed so much.

Momma would say he is just an odd job man doing odd jobs. Odd jobs like house painting, yard work, and the occasional woodwork. Odd jobs sounded about right because he'd be gone coming in and out of the house at all odd hours of the night, waking me up while grunting to himself and making noises. Momma said it was the drink that would get into him, but I didn't know what to make of it. He spent a lot of time in our basement. Working on things Momma would say, woodwork and what not.

I changed out of my pj's and walked into the kitchen, pulling a shirt on over my head. I made my way over to our empty fridge and peered in, grabbing the bottle of orange juice, and then sat at the table looking at Momma. The song on the radio just ended, and I guess they had messed up at the station because there was dead air time that seemed to drag for almost a minute. All that could be heard was the rain hitting our old neglected tin roof. Momma was lost in thought, looking at a puddle that was forming on the kitchen floor next to her from the dozen roof leaks we would have scattered about the house when it stormed. Momma never had enough pots or pans to catch them all.

"Momma? What you thinking?" I asked. She looked up at me. Her eyes were tired and black around the edges from lack of sleep and cigarettes mixed with drinking habits. Those habits had already cut deep lines in her face from her dedication.

"Baby, don't worry about it now. Get your breakfast," she replied.

She had a few hours ago, made eggs and bacon and placed a plate at the table for me. Since Poppa was out, she had let me sleep in. Loved my momma for those types of things. The food was cold, but I shoveled it down. As I gnawed on a cold piece of bacon, I stared at the stain mark on the wall above the kitchen sink where a crucifix once hung. Momma had taken it down after my brother drowned.

"Momma, where's Poppa?" I asked.

"He's out. He went to the hardware store, I believe, baby, to get somethin' for some job he got."

I looked out then at the rain falling off our roof like a waterfall. "Kinda raining hard. I figured he'd be here than go out in that stuff," I said.

"Mind your business and just eat your food," she said, shutting me up.

I ate in silence and listened to the distant thunder. We lived in Gilbertson. My parents were born and raised here and had known of each other but finally met one night at the local dancehall beer joint outside of town. My poppa was a ranch hand at the time to a local rancher, and Momma had just got out of high school. They hit it off immediately.

Heck, they hit it off so well they conceived my brother right there in his truck that night they met.

As we sat in silence together eating, I was jolted out of my thoughts by a steady thud sound coming from the middle of the hallway. It was consistent and got louder.

Momma showed no reaction to it and kept looking at the puddle on the ground. Suddenly the door from the basement in the middle of the hallway swung open, and Poppa stepped out. He was drenched from head to toe for some reason, like he'd been out already. Poppa turned and locked the basement door with his keys he kept on his hip. It was customary for him to do so. I was never to go down there. Poppa made sure I knew that too. He entered the kitchen slowly, never making eye contact. Poppa went to the fridge and popped a beer while grabbing a dish towel and sitting down at the table facing away from us and staring out the window. It was normal for Poppa to have beer for his breakfast. We sat in silence again.

I looked over at him. I could see fresh cuts and bruises blanketing his hands and forearms. It was common for daddy to beat my momma, but this morning, I was confused. Momma had no matching fresh ones to match daddy's fresh ones.

I broke the silence and decided to press my luck.

"Poppa, you think when school gets out next week, I could go to my classmate Daniel's vacation bible school thing at his church? It's free. They got a new playground, and they will have crafts going, and we can..."

"Hell no," he said, cutting me off abruptly.

"Why not?" I asked timidly. He took a long pull of his beer and turned to me. I saw that evil fleeting gleam in his eye as he stared back at me. "Church ain't for nobody but the weak. You gonna get nothin' out of that except a bunch of crap and fill your head with a bunch of random nonsense that ain't true, boy."

"Poppa, please? It's only a week, and I..."

"No!" He said, cutting me off. Mom put out her cigarette and spoke up, "Oh, come on, Clement, the boy needs to do something this summer and he ain't gonna..."

"I said no, dammit!" He slammed his beer down. We sat silent. Poppa leaned into Momma from across the table and spoke in a deep, slow voice. His bloodshot eyes turned even redder, "Don't ever speak over me like that, Darla. You will do what I say, or you know what will happen." Poppa then turned to me. "Get outside." Just like that, he grabbed my shirt and twisted it, yanking me out of my chair. My mother began yelling obscenities and my dad made a beeline to the front door, and without realizing it, I was tossed out the back kitchen door into the ocean in the backyard with the door crashing shut behind me.

I got up soaked, the rain stinging my face and backside. I made my way back to the door and looked in the window to see my mom already on the floor, clutching her face. I then saw my poppa making his way with the breakfast skillet of eggs and bacon in hand. He then opened the door to head back down to the basement and was gone. Without thinking, I ran across the lawn in the down pore and bent down to try and look through the ground window slit that peaked into the basement. Poppa had boarded out the window with cardboard, but there was a tear. Through the dime hole, it was hard to make out anything from the heavy rain spatter that had fogged up the window, but I swore I could make out daddy bending over with the skillet with his arm out as though he was feeding. Feeding something.

Chapter 3
Brittany Johnson

I never understood the Golden Girls. Never did. You got three old white girls living together, laughing it up, and all that seems to happen in this show are scenes about who's trying to figure out who ate whose club sandwich or scenes of all of them huddled up in the kitchen of their nice house at midnight wearing their nice silk Moo Moo's pajamas and crying together while holding each other over nothing but white people problems. This particular episode showed them old girls upset because they were not able to go on some exotic trip together because the neighbor's dog died next door...I guess I can't relate. Being a ten-year-old little black girl in a poor black family in the south, I guess I didn't know how to. I am in a whole other world than the Golden Girls; I figured out. Unfortunately, that is the only thing to watch at midnight with 'rabbit ear' cable and having three channels total. It was reruns of the Golden Girls.

Momma and I lived in the project housing in Gilbertson, right by the railroad tracks next to the old Dairy Queen. The train came twice at night. Usually, I'd sleep through both, but occasionally, it would knock a picture frame off my wall waking me up. I'd lay there and watch the lights from the train poke through the old sheets covering my windows and glide and dance over my room's walls and ceiling shining on all the young faces of my daddy, mama, and pappy's pictures that hung on my wall over my bed. My room would rumble and vibrate, and then just like that, everything was still and calm again as the train passed on to the next town. I would then notice my mother's heavy breathing beside me. Sometimes my momma, Bernice, passed out next to me. She never made it to her bed some nights at all. The smell of that vodka on her would be so strong it would get me sick to my stomach, and I would have to go sleep on the couch. I wanted to believe my momma came to my bed after her shift to be with me. I wanted to believe she missed me during work and wanted to just come to lay and be near me, but I knew better. It would just mean she was drunker than most nights and couldn't make it to her own damn bed.

My momma used to work right next door on the other side of the tracks at the Dairy Queen. I could look out the window of my room to see the big shining fast-food sign at night. Those were better days. We couldn't ever afford for someone to watch me when mama or pappy couldn't, but it didn't matter. Momma was working' right next door. She treated it like no big deal. She'd keep the TV on and set me in my new little bean bag that pappy got me alongside a few snacks and my stuffed animals. Momma would then be gone to work the night shift. I'd make sure to go to bed when I was supposed to, but sometimes I'd get lonely or scared and walk over to the Dairy Queen, and she'd scold me for walking by myself, but I knew she was happy to see me. She would even make me a mini blizzard no matter what time of night it was. We'd just sit there and talk and laugh, and I would eat my ice cream. Her shift would be over before we'd know it, and Momma would clean up real quick, and we would then walk home together hand and hand to go snuggle together back in our little apartment. Yep, those were the better days with Momma. Momma wasn't drinking as much in those days.

She didn't drink at all when daddy was alive. My momma and daddy had known each other growing up. They lived two doors down from each one another in a row of project houses, or huts as daddy would always joke, right on the flood plain next to the Guadalupe River that ran at the very southern tip of town. It was called by the older white generation community up north of town as the slave district by the river or "cotton alley," as the old white people would joke. It was the houses filled with what were once the plantation workers of the south over a hundred years ago. The descendants of the cotton fields and plantations that used to lay scattered amongst the cattle ranches in this part of the surrounding counties came to settle here by the river where it cuts sharp heading for the Texas Gulf Coast. The black neighborhood, over the years, had seen its fair share of challenges and floods. Back in the early 1950s, the KKK movement that was going strong then in the region had set fire to the whole riverside district. Many black lives were lost and many of the houses were burnt to the ground. My grandmother, mama, would tell me later when I was older, that her daddy had been hung that night in their front yard. She and her family had all fled to the woods that very night when they saw the white-sheeted horsemen approaching, but her daddy stayed with pride to protect the home. That next morning when my mama and her siblings returned to a neighborhood of ash, she saw her daddy swinging from the old oak tree that stood in front of where their house once was.

Daddy and Momma's parents both ran a restaurant joint together right down the street from their neighborhood district. It wasn't much but really a shack with a kitchen in back and no air conditioning but a few fans that would blow hot air in the summer. The white people and downtown business folk would line up though come lunchtime.

Momma would say that she and Daddy would laugh while bussing plates at all the older plump white men being lawyers and bankers, in their heavy business suits sweatin' all over the table while they filled their mouths with the best-fried chicken and Guadalupe catfish ever to touch their lips. The 1998 flood came and swept away the place and their houses, however. I was a toddler when it happened, and we went to live with pappy and mama for a while. It was around then, however that daddy asked Momma to marry him finally, and we moved to our own house that we rented. Daddy got a job with the street department for the city, and Mom had started at the Dairy Queen.

I was a lot younger, but I remember my daddy's big hands and arms as he would come home and give me those big deep hugs every evening after working a gravel truck all day. It's those hugs that stay with you. You know that when you get one. It is a hundred percent real and genuine from beginning to end. When he hugged me, he smelled of sweat and tar, but I didn't care. Those hugs would never get old, and I miss them every day. Daddy worked a lot, including overtime, so we could pay our bills, Momma would say, but he always made time for us. Soon daddy started coming home later and later. Momma played it off like it never bothered her, but I could tell it did. One night daddy didn't come home at all, and I woke that morning to Momma and daddy yelling in the living room. That was the beginning of the end of our family together, I think. Daddy got hit by the first-night train that following evening coming home. We didn't live where we are now. We lived in a house that daddy paid for. After he died though, the only place we could find and afford is where we are now. Looking out my window I can look out at night and see the spot where they had my daddy's body covered with a white sheet after he got hit. We were that close now. It's those same train tracks that haunt me at night. They let me know what they took from me over and over again. Momma said it was an accident, but I would find out later drugs were to blame for my daddy's death. He had found a bad influence at work and got hooked.

I raised the remote and clicked off The Golden Girls. The living room went dark but as my eyes adjusted the room then became illuminated by the redness glow of the Dairy Queen sign right down the street. Our apartment was mostly empty and had the faint smell of mold and mildew. Momma wasn't one for cleaning on her time off. There was hardly any furniture except my TV chair and an old ratty couch that was my pappy's and mama's twenty years ago that had been dying a slow death in our living room ever since. Momma never did hang pictures, and our walls were bare. I could hear the first-night train whistle way off in the distance, slowly making its way to Gilbertson. I got up from my now musty and faded bean bag TV chair, which had a huge duct tape strip now running along one side to keep it from busting open, and looked at the clock on our kitchen oven. It was 1:30 in the morning, and Momma hadn't made it back from her shift yet. A year back, the Dairy Queen fired my momma. Apparently, you can't take a free meal home with you every night, or it catches up with you. She pleaded with Caroline, the heavy-set manager with the bursting personality, but it was no good.

Momma didn't work for a few weeks, but then one of my mama's old church friends was able to get Momma a job as a waitress at the all-night diner on the other side of town.

That is when her drink started. She wasn't making as much money, and she would stay behind a few nights out of the week after her shift and drink with the cooks.

Setting the remote down, I shuffled to my room and laid there and looked up at the ceiling. I could hear the train getting closer now. It wasn't but a minute that had passed when I could hear my mom attempting to open the apartment door. I could tell just by how she was fumbling with her keys and fiddling with the lock that she was drunk tonight. She came in, losing her balance and knocked off all the fast-food leftovers that were mine off the counter, making a loud clatter all over the floor. I heard her body slip and hit the ground. She then let out a huge burst of laughter that I am sure woke the neighbors. I could hear then a chain reaction of apartment neighbor dogs next door begin to start barking through the walls. I burned with anger.

Without thinking, I flung my sheets off of me and burst my bedroom door open to see her laying on the ground rolling around still chuckling to herself. "Momma!

Momma! What the hell is going on?! It's late!"

Momma rolled over on her stomach looking up at me. "Don't you be cussin' at me, Brittany J," she said loosely.

"Got to bed," I said as I turned and headed back into my room and slammed the door behind me. The train outside was now approaching, and the whistle began to blare. The low rumbling and shaking of our little apartment started up like clockwork.

Seconds later, Momma opened the door and staggered into my room like a zombie in the dark. She poured into my bed getting on top of me and began cackling like a bird. I didn't find it funny at all. My bed began to shake as the train rumbled by.

"Get off me, you stupid drunk!" I said as I flung her off me. She popped right back up and slapped me hard across the face, half knockin' me off the bed. "I told you to watch that mouth, Brittany J! It be getting you in trouble!" she barked back at me. I touched the side of my face and looked straight back up at her.

"What do you know about anything, Momma? You're just a drunk. If daddy were here, he'd be sad about you and take me away from here."

That was all Momma needed to hear. She closed her fists and began to beat me all over. She beat me to a pulp. No one could hear my screams and pleas over the roar of the first-night train swaying by blowing its horns. She finally wore out after a minute or so and I was able to scramble out from under her sitting on the floor, propping myself up against the wall across from my bed. We both sat in the dark huffing to catch our breath. I wiped blood away from my nose. We sat there in silence for a while. I could still hear the train whine at me in the distance. I thought about daddy. Maybe he was on that train, and I had missed him. I had missed him, and he was right there passing by to take me away from Momma.

More minutes had passed, and Momma was breathing steadily now. I took my blanket from off the floor and hobbled into the livin' room and laid on the couch curling up. Maybe being a Golden Girl wouldn't be so bad after all.

Chapter 4
Kristen Brooks

Living in a cul-de-sac is like living in a bubble. At least, it felt like that for a little privileged white suburban girl that lived in one. I was ten years old going on sixteen. I didn't know my parents; I was already boy crazy and had started my period already last Wednesday. I was born and raised in the little city of Gilbertson, Texas in the arc of the gulf coast that lies south of Houston. Gilbertson was like a train station or an airport. People were just passing through on the way to their final destination when coming to live here. The real locals that had stayed or had generations here were few and far between. Most of the surrounding land in our county was old ranching land or farm land. In the '80s, once the industrial plants started to move in on the nearby coast, we started having more a professional business scene move in. My family was a product of the new professional business wave that came to town. Ross, my younger brother, and I lived with our parents in a new suburb that was built a few years back on the Northeast side of town. It was late summer in 2005, and I was bored sitting in my room. So bored. It was the dead part of the summer now, where everything that was supposed to happen to you that summer already had come and gone. My brother and I went to summer camps, sports camps, and I had stayed over at my friends' houses so many times now that I was now sick of my friends. It was so hot outside during this time of year in south Texas. I felt like if you went outside between the hours of 10 am and 7 pm, you would evaporate.

What also kept us trapped in our own homes that summer was the abductions that started in our county and the surrounding ones. In the past six months, four girls had been abducted and labeled missing. The local law enforcement had active investigations going but had no solid leads at the time. My parents were concerned but not concerned and just told us we had to stay indoors for the remainder of the summer. I'll never forget the one afternoon these abductions hit especially home to me that actually did send a feeling of fear through me. It had been one day after school and my brother, and I had gotten home and were snacking on the couch watching Saved by the Bell reruns as we always did. Suddenly a special news bulletin alert came flashing on the screen showing a bright-eyed brunette girl with freckles about my age that was labeled as missing. I recognized her instantly. It was Debbie Benson. She was from the next town over and had been my bunkmate at camp the past two years. She was a sweet girl who didn't speak much but always showed me love and attention on those few days I was homesick at camp. She had been last seen at her school after hours.

The story was later revealed her parents were late picking her up, and she had decided to walk the mile home and was never seen again.

With all the stories of the abductions going on and fresh on people's minds, school was right around the corner and only a few weeks away, and I was already getting nervous. I was going to be in sixth grade and turning eleven soon. It was a big change from 5th grade. It was middle school, and I found out last week I had Danny Woods in my homeroom when I got my class schedule in the mail. That alone was keeping me up at night. He was my first real crush. Danny was in my grade and had moved to Gilbertson last year. He was a star baseball player who was tall and piercing blue eyes. I knew I was in love. I couldn't help it. Hopefully, this year he would notice me and talk to me, and we would finally be something. I could dream, couldn't I?

I rolled over on my bed and set aside my Danny Woods love drawings on my notebook that were part of my new school supplies for the coming year. Several young bronzed boys with frosty tip hair and pouting lips decorated my wall over my bed. I was some what of a boy band fanatic but never had been to a concert. My parents said it was not on their schedule, nor was I old enough. I wasn't sure if my parents knew how old I really was to be honest. At least, that's what it felt like.

I opened my bedroom door to see a nerf dart whiz in front of my face zipping down the hallway. "Ross!" I screamed. I poked my head back out into the hallway slowly to see my younger brother by two years sitting on the couch in the upstairs den room, looking at me with a devilish grin. He had his

PlayStation on and dozens of nerf guns and ammo rounds flooded the floor at his feet.

"What took you so long to come out? I was aiming for your neck." He said with a giggle. "Ross!" I screamed as I bolted down the hallway toward him.

After taking five more nerf bullets to the body in my pursuit, I reached my brother and tackled him. We both broke into laughter, and I pinned him down, tickling him for two solid minutes until he was threatening me with tears that he had peed his pants. I loved Ross. We were close to a brother and sister that were also close to the same age and constantly stuck with each other. He was very witty for an eight-year-old boy, and he was always down for an adventure and a little trouble but at the same time had the biggest heart in the family. We were also close just for the fact that for the most part, it was really just he and I.

Our parents met at college. They are the typical frat boy meets sorority girl love story. They both had met at an ivy league Christian university. Marriage and family were just another bullet point on the resume in the pursuit of their career goals. Dad got a business degree but was offered out of college a job with an insurance agency and actually liked it and had a knack for sales as he discovered. Mom, too was a business major and had gotten her realtor license and followed dad after their wedding to Gilbertson, where dad was promoted to sales manager of the insurance office branch here. Two years later, they had me and officially set roots and bought a house. Two years later, Ross came by mistake and thus the Brooks family was now complete.

I got up off my brother. He was breathing hard and red in the face. He also was a liar because he had not peed his pants like he had threatened. "Is Mom or Dad coming home early tonight, or are we doing pizza again?" my brother asked. Pizza was our regular meal. It was a treat if mom made it home early with different take out and or groceries to actually cook something. It was kind of the theme at our house. Ross and I were the afterthought. To say that my parents were workaholics is an understatement.

Dad was driven by insurance premium number goals to achieve with his ongoing new clients, while Mom wanted her name on the big billboard on main street once again for the fifth straight year. It would read: "Stephanie Brooks: Our Gilbertson Realtor of The Year!" We would drive by it every morning when mom was taking Ross and me to school. My mother would do the same reaction every time we passed it. She would be on her cell phone yapping away but would suddenly freeze in mid-sentence while slowing down the car to look at it and inspect. Like she expected something to be wrong or for it to read something different this very morning that would deflate or derail her from being number one in Gilbertson. By now, Ross and I had grown used to being on our own and drowned out by our parents' ambitions.

We both were nodding off in the living room watching TV when jarred awake by the headlights and sounds of our parents' cars both pulling into the garage. We met our parents halfway coming into the kitchen. They both were chuckling to each other as they came in. They were obviously a few cocktails in.

"Hey guys, you all eat something?" Mom asked, setting down her purse and some paperwork on the counter. I looked up at the clock above my mom's head on the kitchen wall that read 9:30. Dad passed by, hardly looking at us on the way to his bedroom to change while staring at his cell phone.

"No, Mom. We didn't know if you all were coming home or what the plan was," I said. My brother sat down at the kitchen bar folding his arms.

"Could have called us," Ross mumbled.

"So you guys have eaten nothing then uh?" Mom asked impatiently. "No," I replied. I was wanting her to feel guilty, but that had soared over her head.

Without missing a beat, mom opened up the freezer door and looked inside. "Okay, well...let's see what I can drum up for you guys," mom said awkwardly. Ross and I both sat silently in the kitchen as mom dug through the freezer like an archaeologist trying to find gold and avoiding eye contact because I was laying it on pretty thick. "Here we go! Southwest-style burrito pockets. Yummm!" mom said encouragingly. I rolled my eyes, and Ross yawned.

Dad came into the kitchen in his robe, breaking up the awkward moment. Dad made his way to the counter and still had not made eye contact with me. I was longing just for a glance from him. Just recognition I was there in his presence. Going back, that had always been the history with him and I. He never was really there. He was always looking ahead at what was next in either work or leisure for him. He was never truly present with his kids, and I had recognized that from an early age. The moment even at ten that I wish I could relive over and over again, is the day he hugged me. The day he genuinely showed his love for me. When I was six, I was riding my bike in our cul-de-sac when I took a nasty spill and had cut up my knee pretty badly. Mom was not there and had been showing a house for work that day. Dad was supposed to be watching my brother and me, but Dad was inside working and letting me and my 4-year-old brother run free outside as long as we did not leave our cul-de-sac like he instructed. Pretty trusting, I have to say.

After my body collided with the concrete, I got up and ran inside with my brother bringing up the rear with a curious look of concern on his face. I remember being terrified at all the blood that I saw gushing from my leg. My dad was in the middle of a conference call but quickly hung up, embarrassed and angry at the extreme noise I had made when entering the house. His knee jerk reaction was to start yelling at me as to what was going on, but once he approached me coming around the hallway corner, he then saw the hurt in my eyes. I was pleading with him to make the hurting stop. He took a beat, looking at me being helpless, but then immediately scooped me up and carried me to the bathroom, where he sat me on the counter, cleaning my wound and then bandaged it. Afterward, he held me. He just held me. He cradled me there in his arms in our downstairs guest bathroom for ten long minutes as I whimpered, and just held me.

Little Ross sat right next to us on the floor, holding my hand and singing a song to me in his little voice that he had learned at school earlier that day. I cherish everything about those ten minutes.

Now four years older, I was staring at my occupied dad in the kitchen, thinking of that moment. "Dad?" I said out of the blue, just wanting to get his attention. He finally turned from looking at his phone and glanced up at me. "Hi, sweetheart," he said as he gave me a half-hearted pat on my shoulder. He then turned and made his way around the counter into the kitchen to help my mom get this dinner for their kids over and dealt with so we could be off to bed and out of their hair.

Minutes later, I was staring at a still half-frozen Southwest microwave burrito sitting on a plate in front of me. Most of the lights had been turned off by mom. I could hear my parents in their bedroom down the hall gossiping and giggling to themselves as they recapped their accomplishments of the evening at the work social they had just attended. Ross sat quietly across from me while wolfing his burrito down. I got up and went and set my plate in the sink. I said good night to Ross and went upstairs. I hadn't even made it to the top of the stairs when I started wiping tears away. I shut my door and plopped on my bed, pulling my covers up tight. I laid there and stared blurry eyed out my window down, at the street-lit cul-de-sac below. I thought of that day when I fell. I could see from where I lay in my bed the exact spot I had fallen and wondered if I fell again would my dad be there to hold me.

Chapter 5
Cal Sullivan

Bored to death, I poked holes with my fork through the bottom of my tin foil TV dinner that Momma had made for us. We sat there and ate in silence together, scraping away at our easy ready-to-make microwave meal. It was another day that Momma stayed in her bathrobe. She also hadn't left the kitchen table today and had gone through two packs of cigarettes. I could tell something was weighing on her mind. More than usual anyhow. Charlie Brown Christmas Special could be heard on the Television playing softly down the short hallway from our living room. Momma wouldn't let me eat in front of the TV for fear that dad would walk in and see.

We hadn't had a Christmas tree in years. Dad had either been too busy working or thought it useless to bother with one. As luck would have it, though, Momma was cleaning out the house closets last week and happened to find our old fake four-foot tree in the back corner under a bunch of Momma's collective junk she couldn't let go of over the years. Momma caught Poppa throwing it away in the trash and yanked it out and had then hid it in her own closet over the past few months she later told me. She surprised me a week ago by putting it up. I woke that morning to Poppa and Momma screaming at each other. Poppa then suddenly burst into my room and threw the whole tree on my bed with me half awake. I caught a couple of fake branches to the face that had scrapped my cheek. It about scared me to death. He then slammed my bedroom door shut, and I could begin to hear my mom scolding him. He answered back by shoving her to the floor. At least, that was what I could make out by the sound of it all. I opened my door slowly and then rushed over to help my momma off the ground. She wiped her tears, looking the other way, trying to hide her hurt. She then latched on and hugged me. We hadn't hugged in months. I really couldn't remember when it was the last time we did. I could hear Poppa rev up his truck engine outside after a few false starts and then peel away.

The strand of lights that we had got for the tree years back had only half the lights working now, but as I sat there and ate my TV dinner, I took in how it shined so bright next to Charlie Brown in the living room. Prettiest damn thing I ever saw. Momma had gotten that tree I remember at our mall on sale. It had been before my older brother had drowned. I can still picture the images of my brother huddled over the new tree placing lights and decorations with Momma being her little helper. For me as a two-year-old, the tree stood 60 feet tall, it seemed like. Poppa kept having to pull me away from scattering the decorations everywhere and would tickle me to death as a punishment. There was life in my poppa's eyes then. After my brother passed on, the tree went away. Everything changed after that Christmas.

I got up from the table and put my TV tray in the trash. Mom lit another cigarette, and I filled my glass again with milk from the fridge.

"Not too much baby; we got to have milk for the week," Momma warned.

I brought my glass back to the table and sat down, looking out our side kitchen window across the open lot that sat next to us. I could make out over the old oak trees at the far end of the lot the Catholic church steeple sticking up and lit with light. It shined from a distance, almost angel-like. It was Christmas Eve, and Poppa was out again.

Momma had said he was out doing a job and would be home later tonight. It had been the same way the past several years. Poppa would be out, and Momma and I would be left to fend for ourselves. TV dinners and cigarettes for the holidays.

Momma had already the previous year told me about Santa, so I wasn't looking for him. Santa was always light on the presents anyhow. I drank my milk quietly and continued to look out at the lit-up church steepled through the window. Poppa grew up never going to church, but Momma came from a dedicated catholic family. It was convenient being right down from the church. A few years back, Momma and I would always walk together to mass. We would talk about the sermon together, and I would ask questions about what I heard. I remember as a young child, all four of us would walk as a family to midnight mass on Christmas eve night. I remember how quiet it was on our night walks to and from church. The neighborhood was still and quiet except for a few curious dogs barking at us every so often. We would watch the Christmas lights go by in people's yards, and I would see the families gathered together in their lit-up homes celebrating. I remembered smelling the bourbon on my poppa's breath from Christmas Eve dinner festivities as he carried me to church. It was a year or two after my brother died that we stopped going to church most Sundays but only Christmas and Easter until finally, we stopped going altogether.

I remembered Tommy Woodrow in my class at school was talking the other day something fierce about midnight mass this year and how they were using a real baby in the manger scene that would play out to the congregation before the mass started. It was Tommy's baby brother. Tommy stressed that he didn't know how this evening was going to pan out due to Tommy's little brother, who had apparently had a bad case of the diaper runs for the past week. "It could get messy up there," he said to me nervously on the playground. I not only missed Christmas mass, but this potential tragedy was something I just had to see.

I drained the last of the milk from my glass and set it down. I looked to see Momma staring out the window now at the lit-up steeple sitting across from me. "Momma?" I asked. She looked at me suddenly like she was snapping out of a daydream. Probably dreaming like I did of our night walks to mass, I reckon. "Yes, baby what is it?" Momma replied. She reached again for her cigarette pack.

"You think Poppa be mad if we went to midnight mass tonight?" I asked. Momma looked over at me with tired eyes that got even more tired now that I had mentioned mass. "Cal, we haven't gone in years. Why you wanna go now? You know your daddy wouldn't allow it, and it's ten-thirty now. I wouldn't have time to get ready or…"

"We have time, Momma!" I said, interrupting. "I can get ready real fast and put on that new shirt you got me, and we can go, come back, and Poppa won't even know we be gone." Momma took a drag and exhaled, staring at me with hurt eyes. I knew she wanted nothing more but to go, but it would be the war she would have to face with Poppa to do so. Poppa, from what I knew never exactly had hate for God or mass or even Christmas. However, in the past couple of years, I saw that change. Something had come over Poppa. It had him occupied. It was as though he was now a robot possessed by only himself. Momma and I, as far as I could tell, were not on his radar. God certainly wasn't. Why there would be times recently when I'd get up in the middle of the night thirsty and make my way to the kitchen sink, the whole house would be pitch dark as I would tiptoe to the kitchen to turn the sink on. And as usual, I'd see Poppa out back sitting in his truck with the engine running, talking and yelling at himself. Practically beating on himself. It was beyond eerie. I'd then lay awake after I'd filled my glass to then listen to dad make his way back inside and pace the hallway while breathing heavily. It sounded like a werewolf or something was wandering the house. I'd put my blankets over my head and pray most nights he wouldn't enter my room. I'd then listen to him going in and out the basement most nights as well. The door would open and then shut so many times to that basement before I would finally drift back to sleep.

As Momma and I stood there in the kitchen, I could faintly hear Poppa's truck rumbling down our neighborhood street. He was coming home now. We had a minute before he would be bursting through our back kitchen door. Mom lit another cigarette, and I stared at her, wanting her to fight for tonight.

"Please, Momma. I wanna go. I don't care what Poppa says," I barked. She looked at me and froze. She could see my determination. For the past couple of years now, Poppa has held our house in quiet fear. Momma and I walked around on what felt like eggshells all day to avoid Poppa's foul mood and wrath that came with it. I was tired of it. I was tired of the way our house was at Christmas and frankly tired of looking at my mom in the face at the kitchen table and seeing the same look of doom. I wanted it to be different tonight.

"You gonna get Cal whatever comes to you if you push it with him. I wouldn't ask him if I were you. I'd leave it alone, please," Momma said as she ripped on her smoke with a look of concern. Poppa's truck door slammed, and seconds later, the back kitchen door burst open, entering Poppa's. He made his way to the kitchen sink while shedding his flannel shirt off that was drenched with sweat , as he tossed it in the trash. I looked at Momma, confused. She didn't look phased. He turned and stared at us, looking back at him and his strange entrance. His fresh flat top crew cut gleamed in the kitchen light above him. Poppa wiped away sweat from his brow with his white underwear shirt he only wore now and locked eyes with us.

"Well, what are you two debatin' about over there? Thought maybe you all would be asleep," Poppa said. Momma and I stayed silent and just stared back at him. He turned his back to us with a sarcastic chuckle and began washing his hands now at the sink. Mom puffed away on her cigarette while studying Poppa. I sat quietly, contemplating making the big ask to him. The clock was ticking before mass was to start.

"Darla!?" Poppa barked as he turned from the sink. "In the oven," Momma uttered right on cue.

Poppa popped open the oven and pulled out his TV dinner with a fork in hand.

Poppa grabbed his bottle of whiskey from the pantry and without saying a word, sauntered down the short hallway and plopped on his chair in front of the TV, immediately changing the channel from Charlie Brown. I looked over at Momma, who was shaking her head at me. I ignored Momma and slid off from my kitchen table chair and slowly made my way to Poppa's chair. The old wooden floor creaked as I tiptoed towards the shadowed figure with the flat top silhouetted by the bright light of the TV that gleamed in front of him.

I crept beside Poppa in his chair just as he was taking a huge pull from his bottle.

He choked his gulp down and began picking away at his food tray once again. "What boy?" he said, already knowing I was beside him.

"Poppa, I was wondering if me and Momma could go to church tonight? To midnight mass? Well, I mean you could come too, of course," I muttered.

There was silence beside the chatter of the TV and Poppa picking at his tray and smacking his lips as he inhaled his food down. "...see we just hadn't gone in forever, and Tommy, my friend in my class, was goin' on about his —
"

Poppa slammed his fork down and gripped his bottle again, interrupting me. "Boy, what do you wanna waste time there for? Uh? Ain't nothing you gonna get there tonight that is worthy of your time. It's a waste." Poppa took a pull of his bottle and coughed it down, grabbing his fork once again.

"Well, I just thought it'd be nice to go as a family," I mumbled.

"Not another word, Cal," Poppa said. I didn't let up.

"Yeah, but Dad, we can go and be back, and you wouldn't..."

"I said NOT another word!" Poppa barked. I turned away, walking back to the kitchen table, mumbling to myself.

"I don't know what the big deal is. It's just church…" and with that, Poppa flung his tray at the TV and rose while all at once snatching me by the back of the shirt and lifting me up, pinning me up against the wall by my throat. I started to gasp and cough for air.

Poppa leaned in close to my face. His bloodshot eyes glared a hole in the back of my head. "…Just church, boy? Just church, eh?" I could smell the bourbon as it pierced my eyes, making them burn. It was the same smell from Poppa years ago when he used to carry me to mass all those late nights, holding me as we walked together.

The smell carried a whole new meaning for me now.

"Why of all the nights we wanna go to mass and waste our time? What to hear about Jesus Cal? Is that it?" My face was turning blue. My feet and hands were going numb. I couldn't breathe.

"Let me tell you something Cal, Jesus ain't real, and if he was, then the world wouldn't be the shit place it is, and we'd all be better off. We ain't gonna waste another minute in that place; you got that!?" I was starting to black out. "I said you got that boy!?" he barked. Suddenly, I heard the pump of a shotgun, and a huge black barrel crested against the back of Poppa's neck. He dropped me to the ground and froze. I gasped for air and coughed while looking up to see Momma holding the gun on him. I guess the fake Christmas tree wasn't the only thing she found down in a closet.

"You touch our son again, Clyde, and I am one trigger finger away from messin' up my walls," Momma said sternly. I crawled away and sat on the couch, catching my breath. Poppa turned slowly and stared down Momma. The evil poured from his eyes with his stale glare, and he let out a light snicker of amusement.

"Why…you wouldn't do anything, woman. You are too weak. We all know that. That's where the boy gets it anyhow," Poppa said.

"Try me, Clyde," Momma muttered.

Poppa backed away slowly, turning to head for the basement door. "Fine. Ya'll do what you like. Tell God hi for me. Tell him I'll see him at judgement day." Poppa opened the basement door and exited downstairs..

Momma raised the shotgun to her chin, pointing the gun at Poppa once again. "No, Clyde, you ain't goin' down there tonight. It's Christmas Eve. I won't stand for that. Not tonight with all that mess," Momma warned.

Poppa stared at her and then began to laugh to himself. He moved slowly toward her but stopped and scooped his bottle off the ground. He began to laugh more as he made his way to the back kitchen door. He took the last pull left of the bottle and slammed against the kitchen wall behind him, shattering bottled glass across the floor. Momma and I sat then in silence both breathing heavily as we listened to Poppa laugh insanely now as he got into his truck. His truck engine revved up, and he peeled out.

Momma and I went to the window and watched Poppa's headlights go in circles as he did donuts in the open lot next to our house, defying us. Taunting us. I was scared. If Momma was scared, she hid it well. Then just like that, he was gone.

I swept up the glass off the floor and watched as Momma busied herself making hot cocoa to try and lighten the mood on Christmas Eve. I paused then when I saw her pour the cocoa into one of Poppa's thermoses. She then looked up at me.

"Grab your coat, Cal. Let's get out of this house. It's Christmas Eve, for heaven's sake." We both then smiled at each other.

Minutes later, we were walking down our dark street together, sipping cocoa and heading towards the illuminated steeple where our midnight mass was already in motion. We didn't go in but found a park bench on the curb across the street and plopped down on it together. We sat in silence, looking up at the beautiful cathedral lit up as we sipped hot cocoa together from our thermos. The beautiful nativity scene of the crowd at the manger gathered around baby Jesus lay spread out on the front church lawn.

"You think Jesus really came, Momma?" I asked, breaking the silence.

"...I'm not sure anymore, Cal. I used to think so. I don't know anymore," Momma said, trailing off in thought. Momma then handed me back the cocoa thermos to tend to some tears in her eyes. I scooted over when seeing this, and we wrapped our arms around each other. The front church doors opened across the street, and the congregation began to bustle out into the night air.

"Cal, I'm so sorry. ...I am sorry it's like this." Momma had a tortured look on her face. It was the most emotion I had seen on her face in years. I held her tightly.

"Momma, it's alright," I assured her.

"No, it's not. You shouldn't have to witness all that at the house," she said. "Your father…" Her voice started to crack as the tears started coming again. "I can't take it…Your daddy's got them down there…"

Tears overcame her as she broke down. I hugged Momma tighter.

"Got what? What does Poppa get?" I asked. Momma then wiped her face well and stood up, breaking her moment of weakness.

"Come on," she suddenly blurted out. "Let's get on home," she said. We walked home together in silence, staring at the Christmas lights strung on all the old houses as we passed them. My mind was heavy. I knew by what Momma said to me tonight, she was trapped. I just never knew the depth of it.

Momma, later that night, tucked me in and assured me it would be okay. "It'll be fine, baby. No matter what is going to happen that I love you. I would never let him hurt you, Cal," she assured me. She then told me she would sleep with me in my bed tonight.

The shotgun too. I drifted to sleep for a while, but then something stirred me back awake. I sat up to see I was alone in my room, and Momma was not there. The smell of something good was coming from the kitchen. What was Momma doing? I eased out of bed and pushed my door open slightly, and poked my head out. Momma had cooked a meal, and I could see her carrying a plate to the basement door. She opened it and began down the stairwell. I moved and stood at the top of the stairs staring down into the darkness, and called to her.

"Momma, what you doin'?" I asked.

She turned around, startled at the bottom of the stairs, and looked up at me. "Cal!…You scared me. Go back to bed, baby. I don't want you down here."

I looked at her, confused. "Go, Cal. This won't take long. Go get in bed, and I will be there in a minute. Go!" she commanded. I slowly shut the basement stairwell door and stood there perplexed for a moment. I shuffled back to my bed and laid there. My mind stretched in every direction. My clock read 3:30 am. Merry Christmas, I told myself.

Chapter 6
Brittany Johnson

I woke the next morning to our apartment phone ringing in the kitchen. I had a feeling it had been ringing in the kitchen for a while. I sat up from the wall in my room. I had fallen asleep laying upright all night. I must have drifted off, staring at my mother in that drunken comma. My back was stiff and ached as I looked to see that she had not moved at all and was in the same position that she had passed out in.

I got up and wiped the dry, crusted blood away from my cheek and side of my eye from last night. I opened my bedroom door and made my way to the phone on our kitchen wall that was still going crazy.

"Hello?" I said faintly, still getting my bearings. It was pappy. He had called like he usually does on Sunday mornings to see if Momma and I were alive and needed a ride to church. The answer was always the same.

"Hey, pappy! Yeah, we comin'. You know we comin! ...Momma still in bed, so we'll see. ...Okay, see ya'll in a bit. Love you too."

I hung the phone back on the wall and looked at the oven clock. I had thirty minutes before pappy and mama would come by in their old clunker of a Cadillac and pick me up. For the past two years now, Pappy and Mama would make the two-minute drive from their old house by the river to come pick me up and take me to their old all black Baptist church back down by the river in the black section of town here in Gilbertson. As mentioned, it was the section of town known to flood. The flood district they labeled it. Funny how the flood district usually is the black district. To lose your house or business was a common thing when mother nature did not play nice. We all knew that by now.

My grandparents' church had been there for over a hundred years and had flooded three times but was still standing on its foundation. Much less it had been attempted to be burnt down by the clan too that fateful night my great grandpappy was hung in that tree. Pappy would say God's grace was sealing it off from the river's wrath. Pappy always talked about grace, come to think of it. From what I saw, God hadn't given my pappy a whole lot of grace. He was an orphan by age seven, had all but broken his back in hard manual labor all his life with not much to show for it, and out of his five children all had died over the years before him except my Momma who was well on her way if you asked me. I looked up to pappy because given all his hardship, he still claimed to give God the glory. He was thankful for what he did have, but it wasn't really that much at all as I saw it. Mama was the same and fell right in line with my pappy's disposition. That's what made them so attractive in my mind, I guess. It was their humbleness. It was their attitude I was also jealous of. All the nights over the years I stayed at my grandparent's little shack on the river, I never saw their attitude change. I never saw them be ugly to one another. We always prayed together before our meals in that house and knelt at the foot of the bed to pray before bed. I was always fond of holding my pappy and mama's hands when we did pray. A sense of comfort would always come over me when I held their old and brittle hands that felt like sandpaper.

I walked into my bedroom again and stared at Momma. She had not woken and had wet my bed. It has happened time after time. A bit of dry, crusted vomit was beside her head where she lay. Oh, my sweet momma. Luckily Pappy and my mama had taught me to do laundry. It has been coming in handy; lately, I have to say. I could tell I was going to be mad at Momma this morning. More than the other Sunday mornings. It was a different Sunday morning. It was this Sunday that I was to be baptized. I was to give my public vow to the Lord above in front of our little congregation right there behind our little white church in the shallow waters of the Guadalupe.

My pappy and mama's little church had a baptism once a year in the Summer to all those who were to get baptized in the congregation. It usually averaged two or three folks per year. Pastor Tillman, a short heavy-set man with snow-white hair and a toothy smile, would put on his bed sheet-like robe and wade out into those muddy waters of the Guadalupe River, waving his members to wade on in behind him. One by one, they would be dunked and revived again from the waters as now a baptized believer in Him publicly showing a testament as Pastor Tillman would bellow out, of their faith. The small seven-member choir would be out there as well, waist deep and deep into belting gospel hymns as the rest of the congregation clapped and sang along. There was something simple yet timeless about this ceremony that had been going on for decades among our church members. I loved baptism day and today was my turn. It was my turn, and I knew that my momma would not be there to see it. I had known it for a long time though deep down, that she wouldn't.

It was only last year, while sitting on the front doorstep of my pappy's house waiting for my momma to get off work, that my pappy had led me to the Lord. Up until then, I had always heard the bible stories and prayed when told to pray, but I never personally thought about what it was and meant to have a personal relationship with Jesus. That night, after mama had filled me with her fried pork chops and homemade cornbread, I decided to get personal with the Lord once and for all. Pappy extended his old sandpaper hands out and took mine, and led me in a prayer. It was then I knew of his presence, and my relationship with HIM had truly begun.

"Momma, you comin' today?" I asked. She laid there lightly snoring now in my bed. I went over to the edge of the bed and gave her a shove. She rolled over, mumbling light profanities to me, and started snoring again. I went over to my chair in my room, where I had my Sunday dress laid out that my mama had got me a few months back for this day. I slipped my dress on and went into the bathroom to braid my hair. It was only a few years ago, before Momma started drinking, that she would braid my hair every morning before school and church in the living room while I watched cartoons. Now it was just me alone in our small bathroom. The small mirror had two large cracks in it which made my braiding a challenge.

I brushed my teeth and put my dress shoes on at the edge of my bed and then sat there in silence, listening to my mother's breathing once again. A lawn mower hummed outside in the distance coming from down the street. I wonder what it would have been like if daddy hadn't gotten hit by the train. Would he be here now cooking waffles for Mom and I like he used to. We would eat, me not trying to get syrup on my new Sunday dress, and then loading up into daddy's truck all together to go to the church. Momma would be sober too.

I stepped out onto the front porch stoop of our apartment complex and sat there in my dress on the steps, shielding my eyes from the early rising sun. I brought a plastic bag with me with a pair of shirts and shorts for the actual river itself when I was to be dunked in the holy spirit. Mama wouldn't dare have me mess up the dress she got. It had already started to heat up now. That was typical for a midsummer morning in south Texas. We had all grown accustomed to it. I would sweat even more through my dress on the ride over to the church in my pappy's old Cadillac. I never knew to have his Cadillac air conditioner actually work. It just blew hot air all the time whenever I rode in it, but I never minded.

I scanned the street, still shielding my eyes, and turned to see where the lawn mower sound I had heard earlier was coming from. There diagonally down across the street a hundred yards away, I could see an old black Ford ranger truck parked on the street curb in front of another duplex with a lawn in front. A scruffy, dirty-looking young man of maybe nineteen or twenty in faded old coveralls was pushing a mower. Lawn equipment laid sprawled about in his truck bed amongst other junk it looked like. I scanned the other way to see the Dairy Queen had not yet turned on its lights to begin the day and brace themselves for all the churchgoers that would be heading there after church service to get a dip cone or blizzard while gossiping about all the small-town folk that they would be praying for. I noticed the lawn mower engine had cut off now, and I turned back to look. I could see how the man had stopped mowing and stood there in front of his truck staring back at me while wiping his hands with a rag of some sort. He stood there frozen, looking straight at me. After a minute went by, I became uneasy. I started looking around to see if anybody was out witnessing this creepy white man with a staring problem. Nobody was stirring, though. It was still too early. I turned back to see him now in the middle of the street, pacing this way toward me. I stood up instantly and began walking across my apartment lawn in the other direction up the road. My heart began to pump fast, and my fingers became numb. What did this guy want with me? Why I didn't go back to my momma at our apartment, I don't know. I guess I didn't feel safe there.

I turned back and saw he was gaining on me. He smiled now and even gave a short wave back to me as he strode towards me. I broke into a trot and began to whimper in fear. My heart was throbbing now up in my throat. It was then that I heard the most beautiful sound all morning. I looked up to see my pappy's old Cadillac turn the corner in front of me, making its way towards me. It rumbled down the street with exhaust smoke blowing heavily out the back. The side paneling on the passenger side had come unglued and rattled on every pothole my pappy went over. Pappy pulled up, and I leaped inside out of breath. My dress was soaked in sweat as I poured into the backseat. I looked ahead past the front dash to see that the man in coveralls was nowhere to be found. He had vanished. All that remained was the little black truck still parked there as we cruised by.

"Honey, you all wet! What's been going on this mornin'?" Pappy asked me, concerned and wide-eyed, as he peered at me through his overhead mirror. I wiped my brow and turned back to look behind me down the street. He was gone. I turned back to see mama from the front seat and pappy in the mirror looking at me like I just went through a hurricane.

"I'm fine. It's just hot out, is all," I said, brushing it off now that I was safe. My pulse subsided.

Pappy turned left, and we exited onto the highway towards the river. Towards our church. Towards my baptism.

Chapter 7
Kristen Brooks

Ross and I had been waiting in our family suburban with the engine idling in the driveway for a while now. It was Christmas Eve, and this evening had turned into a family tradition of sorts like all families. It consisted of the same mundane events for the past several years now. My brother and myself would beat Mom and Dad dressing for church and then sit in the suburban waiting for them to finish dolling themselves up to then get in the car so we could go down to the local big historic church downtown and be seen once a year by the who's who of Gilbertson as families packed themselves in the pews to hear of baby Jesus. We then would drive home to have Mom's overcooked Christmas roast.

We had been sitting in the backseat for well over twenty minutes. Ross and I both wore church clothes one size too small as mom had yet to take us clothes shopping for this past year. Ross kept to himself, playing on his Gameboy video game pad, and I had in front of me one of my school textbooks I had left in the backseat and was drawing hearts and doodling on the textbook cover wherever I could find space. The initials and name of my love, Danny Woods, covered the book cover like a virus. Sixth grade had been going well for the first semester. I had made the sixth-grade junior high basketball team and had finally got up the courage to speak and flirt with Danny, which had paid off. He seemed to love the extra attention, as it turned out, and we were now an item around school going steady. Of course, all that meant in the sixth grade was I saw him at school, and we would walk around the halls holding hands and sending notes to one another in class when we could. Last Friday, before I got on the bus to go home, I had gotten bold in the bus line, and when I saw the bus line teacher turn her back, I dared Danny to kiss me. He rose to the occasion and did so while holding me close, if but only for five seconds or so. I turned and got on the bus, gushing while watching him stand there with his backpack looking for me through the windows as I found a seat. I was floating as the bus pulled away. It was my Casablanca scene that played out as we broke for the holidays.

The driver seat and front passenger doors opened, and Mom and Dad finally got in the car. It smelled like Christmas Eve because dad had his especially musty Ralph Lauren Polo cologne on that he had had forever, which Mom had given him when they first got married. He seemed to only wear it for Christmas eve service too. I was already getting a headache from it. We pulled out of the driveway and backed out onto our cul-de-sac. The houses around our street circle were aglow with Christmas light decor.

Instantly, Mom and Dad both reached for their cell phones. Dad began babbling to a client about their insurance renewals for the new year deadline while mother was making empty promises to an interested buyer for one of her house properties. It was always the same. Communication was lacking as a family, and I always felt Mom and Dad one day, when their career goals would come up short, they would then feel that void and look back on the years and moments missed with their children when they were right in front of them.

Dad turned left, and we went over the railroad tracks passing the Dairy Queen and dirty project apartments that scattered the area. Poverty was something I never knew but saw depending on what side of town I was on. This Dairy Queen happened to be the only one in town which was located in the older section of town. We would go there to get blizzards after Ross's baseball games sometimes when he played at the little league fields just down the road. I remember sitting in the booth there gnawing away at my chocolate chip cookie dough blizzard and looking at all the different colors and races of people that were working there and whom we sat amongst. It's interesting how families of different ethnicities and economic backgrounds would stare at each other and study each other while consuming their DQ ice cream treat in silence. All the different people of Gilbertson would gather there in one place, and it was okay to look at each other to judge or ponder while entranced with your ice cream. It was allowed. It was then in those moments I knew then how thick my cul-de-sac bubble truly was.

Our suburban took a right, and we pulled up to the church in the historical neighborhood district of downtown Gilbertson. The church itself was beautiful but unfamiliar to us, really. We'd only come here twice a year, if that. Once for Christmas Eve service and then Easter if we had my mom's parents in town that year. They were quite the devout church goers. My mom hung up her phone and turned back to look at my brother and me in the backseat. My tight dress itched as I situated my pantyhose and unbuckled my seatbelt.

"Okay. You guys look good," mom said, exhaling as she studied us up and down in the backseat. She truly was looking at us for the first time today. Ross turned his Gameboy off and looked up. "Mom, do we really have to go tonight? It's the same message every year, and it's hot in there. It's lame."

Our dad hung up his cell phone now and turned to look at us, chiming in on the conversation. "Ross, Listen to your mother. We are going in there, and I want smiles," Dad barked.

"Oh, hi, Dad. Thanks for joining us," Ross muttered sarcastically.

"Ross, don't be like that. Let's all go in, say hello to everyone, and it will be over before you know it," Mom said consolingly.

We all exited our car in the best of moods and crossed the street towards the front door of the church sanctuary. The sun was setting low, and I exhaled, seeing my breath as we crossed the street. A cold front had blown in the night before and for south Texas, cold weather was a treat as well as a luxury. Most Christmas eve's it was a nice balmy eighty degrees that would always get you in the Christmas spirit. Father Stevens met us at the front door, ushering us in. My dad shook his hand, and my mother gave him an awkward hug. I could tell Father Stevens knew our faces but couldn't place who we really were. That's how often we attended church.

Dad entered the sanctuary first and immediately went into salesman mode, working the room, extending out his hand to all, and meeting faces with a huge smile and welcome. Mom got pulled away too into being questioned by members of her fellow rotary board club, leaving Ross and I to find seats at our designated pew we all sat at every year. It's funny because I think half of the congregation here this evening were only holiday members that too had their own designated pews for their families each year.

Most of the families I saw sitting amongst us were ones I hadn't seen in a year myself since the last Christmas Eve service we had attended here.

Ross and I found our designated pew that was far back right of the sanctuary, and we took our seats. We sat in silence and watched all the families greet each other. I saw eight pews up in front of me, little James Giddings. He was a wild blond-haired short and stocky kid that was the bully of my grade. He sat there looking back at me, waving with a mischievous grin before his mother sat down next to him, thumping his forehead and making him turn around.

"That kid's creepy," Ross uttered to me, noticing James.

"I know," I said without breaking a beat. We watched our parents for a few remaining minutes, continue the social rounds, and then come and sit beside us, ready to hear the routine Christmas message. Father Stevens took the pulpit that sat perched high above us. Father greeted all of us warmly. He then went on to preach about baby Jesus. He talked about the manger scene and what happened that fateful night amongst the hay and barn animals. I found my mind drifting as I sat in my pew, and I wondered about baby Jesus. Was he real? Was Jesus just another holiday myth like Santa that was supposed to make us all warm and cozy inside? Was there really some virgin in a barn out in the desert thousands of years ago that gave birth to a kid that would be the savior of the world? It all seemed kinda Disney. Kind of far-fetch to me. I had trouble relating, and do we really know what happened back then?…If anything at all. I guess that's why at the end of Father Stevens sermon, he brought it home.

"And that's why it takes faith. Faith in the Christmas story is the best kind of faith. It is faith in a baby coming into the world in the mud and hay of an old barn shack to die for all of us that don't deserve to be. Jesus was a miracle. In order to believe miracles happen or didn't happen, it does take some kind of faith. It is my hope tonight's congregation that you all will trust in that miracle."

An hour and ten minutes had past when the congregation proceeded out of the front church doors into the cool night air. Ross breathed a sigh of relief as we headed to the car. We piled into the car and again, my parents took to their cell phones. Only this time it was too late to be calling clients. It was our family members catching up and wanting to make New Year's plans. Ross and I again sat in the back seat in silence. My brother turned and looked at me, rolling his eyes and putting a finger pistol in his mouth to signal his emotions as our parents rambled on.

We turned into the busy parking lot to get some last-minute grocery items my mom hadn't gotten earlier in the week. Dad pulled into a parking space and shut off the car.

He then went over the grocery list for mom. Mom, however, didn't feel the confidence coming from Dad, and she decided to get out and go with. Ross suddenly wanted a soda, so it now left me sitting alone in the back seat in silence once again. I watched families, and the people of Gilbertson busy their way in and out of the holiday door traffic entering and exiting the grocery store's front entrance.

Suddenly an old black beat-up Ford ranger truck pulled up to the empty parking space aside from our suburban. I watched as the man sat there in his driver's seat, finishing his cigarette and flicking it out the window, hitting the side of our car in the process. He got out and blew his nose with his back pocket handkerchief scanning the parking lot. He made his way to the back of his truck bed and fiddled with the pile of junk and lawn equipment that lay in the bed. He was a younger dark headed man probably in his twenties but his sheepish face had been worn to that of a forty-five-year-old. He had on old dirty coveralls, and I could smell his body odor through the crack in my back passenger window. His teeth were brown and yellow and he carried heavy dark circles under his light blue eyes.

He turned and suddenly noticed me through the lightly tinted window of our suburban staring at him. He gleamed a brown crooked tooth smile. "Well, Merry Christmas," he mumbled. I froze without doing anything while a lump had formed in my throat. I was enjoying my privacy from my family but now wanted them all back in the car with me. Cell phones or not.

He looked around, checking his surroundings again, and then leaned up to the glass sticking his dirty mouth in the window crack. "You're too young to be out here by yourself in the dark, aren't you, little bird?" he said. I could hear the door handle jiggle below him at his waist, trying to open my car door. Dad had done one thing right tonight by locking it. Before I could react, the car door opened on the driver's side, and Dad started to pile a few grocery bags inside the front middle console. I exhaled a deep breath and looked back to see that the man was gone. Vanished. Ross then piled into the backseat beside me.

"What's wrong?" he asked, noticing my face that had gone white. I explained to him what had just happened, but he laughed it off as some kind of joke. I spoke up to mention to dad about the strange man I just encountered, but before I could say anything…his cell phone rang.

Chapter 8
Brittany Johnson

I awoke suddenly, gasping for breath. I instantly hoped I had woken from the nightmare as I lay there. However, I knew when the stale smell of cigarette smoke hit my nose that I hadn't. I was still here. It had been two weeks or so now that I had been taken and living in the basement of the man who was my kidnapper. At least, I think it was two weeks. I was starting to lose track of the days. I am fifteen years old now reported missing. I laid there frozen in his bed, paralyzed and sore from head to toe in all places. I looked up and stared at his dirty fan above me, spinning lazily. He had forced himself on me again, and I had passed out from the fear mixed with the pain that it caused.

My kidnapper coughed violently from the bathroom and hacked something up that quickly shook me. I turned my head towards the beam of light that shined on my face from the crack in his adjoining bathroom doorway. I could see through the crack him standing there naked, looking and mumbling to himself in some language I couldn't make out. I was naked as well but was not tied up at this particular moment. I slowly felt my wrists and winced at my raw skin that had blistered over from the rope he would always tie me with. Only this time, I was free. Is it true? He must have thought I had passed out or was knocked out and not worth tying. I at least had facial bruises to prove it.

Now was my chance. I could rise and make a sprint for his door. I lay there as he hummed to himself in the bathroom and began to quickly picture my escape. It was easy. I would sit up suddenly but without a sound and open his bedroom door, sprinting down his short hallway to the back door and opening it to the sunlight. To freedom, I would sprint to the next house screaming from joy mixed with fear. I would be met with the open arms of a family there. They would have a blanket waiting for me, and I would tell them two more are down there in his basement needing help. The police would be called. Pappy would come. Mama and even Momma would come. We would all hug and cry, and then I would go home. Momma would not even think to drink that night, and she would hold me sober for the first time in years. It would be different. I thought this thought every minute I had been here. I was so close now. When would I get this chance again?

I trembled and shook violently as I began to sit up and slide off the bed to make my escape. Unfortunately, the bathroom door burst open suddenly and I immediately laid back, looking the other way trying not to shake while closing my eyes to pretend I was still out. I could feel his presence as he approached the bed. I could hear and feel his heavy breathing as he leaned over me, stroking my hair. "My little bird," he said eerily. "Thank you." I fought back to keep my body from trembling but was not doing a good job of it. He didn't seem to notice as he reached for my limp wrists to tie them tightly together. He tied a knot around them and yanked hard. The rope burned against my sores, and I couldn't help but scream, and the word came to my mouth as the sheer pain hit me. I couldn't help it. It just came. The word was "Jesus." I don't know why I said it in pain, but I did. I felt the word come from the gut of my soul. From the bottom.

Even though over the past two weeks I thought he, Jesus, had forgotten me and I had forgotten him but yet I still called for him.

My abductor took a beat and stepped back. The word had caught him off guard, and I could tell now it bothered him. He grabbed me violently and with one swipe, threw me across the room into the corner of the wall. I hit the wall and flopped to the ground. It had knocked the wind out of me, and I lay there naked, gasping for breath. For the small, scrawny man that he was, I was surprised by his raw strength. He stood over me once again, beginning to breathe heavily and started to shake and convulse while gibbering away something from his mouth. I looked up to see him suddenly lift, and there in front of me, he was levitating a few inches off the ground, just hovering. I sat up screaming, backing away from him. The darkness around his eyes got even darker. He began to pant and snarl at me like a lion. His feet then hit the ground once again, and he grabbed me and swung me over his shoulder, and took me down the hall towards the basement door. I began to kick and scream. His body was so hot I felt it literally burning my skin. We reached the basement door and began down the stairs to what was now my new home and had been for the past few weeks.

We reached the bottom of the basement stairs, and the commotion had awoken my two other cell mates from their sleep. He dropped me to the dirt floor, hitting my head. I could hear him unlocking my cage. It was a five-foot by five-foot cage of thick metal wire that sat up against the back wall of his basement. The two other young girls that were my fellow prison roommates had their cages across from mine on the other side of the room. I was lifted and shoved inside and discarded like a piece of trash. Like he does every time he is done with me. He shackled my ankle with a chain that connected to one of the main foundation beams of the house that stood right outside by cage. Before I realized it, he was gone. All I could hear now was my breathing as I laid there, inhaling dust particles from the dirt floor. We all three laid there in the dark, quiet, not saying a word. There was nothing to say. I passed out from exhaustion.

It was some hours later I awoke to sirens. I sat up and looked around. I had done this a lot the past few weeks. I would hear sirens, and my heart would leap out of my chest. I thought they were coming. I thought it was the sound of my salvation. I thought that maybe he had been found out, and they were coming to save us three. I would sit there and listen for the door to burst open and then to hear the clashing footsteps heading down the stairs to come get us. But it was the same every time. The sirens would get close, but just like that, they would fade away again to silence, and reality would set in once again. We were alone. I reached over to the corner of my cage and grabbed a rag that had been left for me, and dipped it in my water bowl. I then sat back against my two pillows that were also left there to me, and I treated the fresh wounds on my face. It was dark in the basement except for the natural light of outside street lamps that shone through the cracks of the ground-level basement windows that hadn't been completely covered up. The basement itself was not big. I was guessing it was maybe a twenty by fifteen-foot area. The floor was dirt, and one light bulb hung from the center of the ceiling on a cord; however, it was never really used. Stacks of old boxes filled with particles and fragments of magazines, books, and old dusty and tattered clothes lay scattered everywhere amongst the three designated and occupied cages where he kept us. I could see to my right he had kept boxes stacked high with girls' clothes and artifacts. Most likely my fellow past victims that lived down here. The cages themselves were not flimsy but were also not very fortified. Our abductors sure bet on us attempting to escape through the cages and therefore relied on us trying to pry the two-inch thick chain that wrapped around our ankle off from the one-foot-thick foundation beam that we all three were chained to. The beam towered in the center of the basement room itself.

I looked behind me to readjust the pillows that I was lying against when I noticed something sticking out from the dirt behind me. It was the corner piece of some kind of cloth or fabric that stuck out just inches outside of the graded wiring of my cage. I poked my hand through the wiring and began pulling at the fabric and digging around it, carving it out. Minutes later, I had unearthed a square object wrapped in old cloth that was dirt stained. I fingered away the cloth to reveal an old black leather family bible.

Why was something like this buried in the ground in this basement of all places? I would never know. I would never know that my abductor grew up in this very house and that his momma buried this bible to hide it from her husband and had forgotten about it. It lay buried for decades now until I, some poor little kidnapped black girl, had found it outside her cage.

I noticed something poking out of the top of one of the pages, and I thumbed to it. There I saw an old faded black and white photo of a family of three standing outside of what I could make out was the front of this very house. It was a good-looking white family. The mother was small and petite, wearing a strained smile. The dad towered over the other two standing in the back sporting a flat top hairstyle. The dad's facial expression seemed lost and reserved except for his eyes, which had an intensity to them. I looked then to see the little boy that was sporting a smirk and squinting from the sun in the photo. The boy had to be no more than nine or ten. It was then that I folded the photo and brought it into my cage to get a better look. I stared at the little boy for a long time. I knew him. It took me a moment, but I remembered. I dropped the photo, gasping, and then grabbed it again, studying it. Pure anger came over me. It was him. He was younger in this photo, but it was him. It was the man I saw that day that chased me down the street in my Sunday dress on my baptism day. Now I am here with him. Down here in his basement. I broke down and cried for some time, going through all the emotions all over again anger, fear, dread and then just sadness. I began to think of my pappy. I knew I had to be strong. I knew he would want me to be. I knew that it was no mistake to find this bible in the ground. I knew pappy would want me to have it and use it as my flashlight while down here in the darkness. It was then that I repositioned myself in my little cage and did something that I had not done since I had been taken. It was an instinct. That had nagged at me the day I was shut in this cage but had pushed away down deep. I broke down and submitted it now. I started to pray.

Chapter 9
Kristen Brooks

The back of the bus was bumpy coming back from our weekend basketball tournament in late February of my sophomore year. Everyone knew that the backseat of the bus was where all the good gossip was created and then dispensed out onto campus. It was 2010, and I was on the tenth-grade JV basketball team. I was a sub-par backup point guard, if you want to be completely honest, but I enjoyed it. I had received most of my skills from our long afternoons when Ross and I would shoot hoops on his basketball goal in our driveway, waiting for mom and dad to come home from work or wherever it was that they were. Ross was a natural, even from a young age, and he would only make me better each time we had our late afternoon battles against each other under the infamous hoop.

It was late into the night as our team bus, aka 'the yellow dog' as our coach would nickname it with a certain twang in her east Texas voice, made its way down the lonely south Texas country farm road that I would travel down so many times in my high school basketball career. I sat in the second row from the back fiddling with my new iPod that my parents had gotten Ross and me for Christmas. Most of the girl gossip had died down now that we were into our second hour of the returning road trip. Only people that were left chattering away about boys and or any girl drama were the usual suspects-Stacy Settles and Nicole Burnings. That was typical, though, and I had grown bored of it, and I put my earbuds in to listen to some angst teen girl music for the rest of the ride home.

Stacy, Nicole, and I had been friends since kindergarten. We had gone through the ups and downs of girlhood, from menstrual cycles to boy crushes, training bras, and the damage that girl gossip did to our soul and friendship to boot. The three of us had survived all that but lately, there had been a gap between myself and Nicole and Stacy. Couldn't put the finger on the exact reason why either. I suspected because it was becoming more obvious the social class difference between us the older we had gotten.

Stacey and Nicole had always lived in the gated community. My parents made strides throughout my whole life to get there, but it was just out of reach. They were super proud though I had gated community friends. I was over the girl drama as well. I was interested in talking to boys, and they were interested in talking about boys…that and everyone else's baggage they would make up about everyone. I was over it. In past months, I had slowly drifted away from the gossip circle and thus were losing two close childhood friends because of it. I began now to slowly become more in the market of new girl friendship.

I happen to look up and see two rows in front of me, our newest player that had come onto the team mid-season, Brittany Johnson. She was a short and stocky-built girl with a soft face and eyes. She was standing up, looking back at me as she dug deep into her backpack, trying to find something. She locked eyes with me but quickly turned away, getting back into her seat and facing forward. I felt sorry for Brittany. She was the classic fish out of water. She was one of the few black students we had on our high school campus that had got redistricted from the south side of Gilbertson this past school year. She was quiet, kept to herself, and I could tell she didn't really know how to act around so many white people in one place, most likely. I have, to be honest, I wouldn't have either. She seemed nice though, and was a hell of a three-point shooter and defender under the basket. She quickly in just months' time, was earning a starting spot on the team and you know that got some local parents fired up. I loved it.

Sitting there, this wave of empathy hit me for Brittany. Reputations and rumors had spun around school about her and her home life. No thanks to the Stacy and Nicole of the world. Brittany would often to show up to class or practice with fresh bruises and or cuts on her which never helped extinguish those rumors. She did a tremendous job at hiding them, though. Cuts and bruises on the inside and out, that is. Before I realized it, I was up and making my way down the bus aisle, and before I could blink, I plopped down next to Brittany, half scaring her to death in the process. Besides being empathetic, I don't know what propelled me but maybe just pure curiosity. She was so talented, but nobody ever seemed to speak to her, and it seemed she was never going to be the one to break the ice. I now found myself being the one to break it.

"Well, here's our three-point assassin," I said playfully. Brittany was shocked and didn't know what to say as she stuttered out some words. "Yeah, right...a lotta bricks tonight."

"We've never really talked. What are you jamming to here?" I asked, reaching for her CD case.

I saw that she was still sporting an old 1990s' style CD Discman. She hadn't had the luxury, I was assuming, of upgrading to the iPods of the world. It was fair to say I liked Brittany from the start. She was always cool and calm and went with the flow but beneath it all had an intensity to her that only came out every once in a while, either through joking around or on the basketball court. I didn't know it, but Brittany would change the course of my life forever. A few times in fact. It would be t-minus thirty-one days before we would become fast best friends and it would be exactly ninety-one days from now that Brittany would be abducted and I would forever blame myself for her disappearance.

Brittany chuckled at my observation and commented that we couldn't all have iPods. "Some of us gotta keep it real with the old school," Brittany joked. We both laughed, and Brittany began to open up to me. We had in that particular bus trip another hour and a half to go, and I felt that in that timeline, we covered a lot of bases. We talked about school. We talked about boys, or lack thereof. Brittany admitted to me that she had indeed kissed a boy once. It was at her grandparents' house for a BBQ they were having. Apparently, a boy from out of town that was friends with her cousin was quite the Romeo and laid one on her in the dark shadows amongst the parked family cars after the BBQ that night. We talked about the team and her talents that she would deny.

Brittany was a natural on the court. She carried the ball with ease and had the best court vision on the team. I thought it was crazy when she told me she had only been playing a few years now. It was ever since her little church by the river got a goal given to them as part of this community outreach program in Gilbertson for church youth programs that she started shooting the ball around with some of the other kids from her church. From that point on, she was hooked.

Brittany validated my suspicion that the school change and being redistricted and moved across town had been hard but that she enjoyed the opportunity to play basketball here now. We then got into the subject of family which we found was a dark horse for both of us. I could tell Brittany withheld some. She only wanted to talk about certain aspects of the family, like her grandparents and her church. Even though I could tell there was a lot of hurt there with her mother, I still found myself jealous. I was jealous of the love and community she got from her grandparents and her church. That was one thing I did not have, and I felt I was seeking that out in other ways whether it was with boys' attention at school, the typical partying and drinking, and or the community I found on the basketball team. My parents and my home life was still a void for me. I think Brittany and I shared that void and that's what brought us close.

Chapter 10
Brittany Johnson

I opened up my looker and took a deep breath shoving my geometry book in with force. I hate numbers, angles…all that math has to offer. Sophomore math was going to be the death of me. The third-period school bell had rung and my fellow students flooded the hallway swirling around the backside of me like yellow jackets. I took another deep breath and closed my eyes, exhaling. I listened in silence as the hallway behind me grew louder and louder with the banging of lockers and shouting as the student body made their way past me to their next class.

I was redistricted and had been going to the North Gilbertson high school for the past four months and still felt as though I was on an island. I was a black ship stuck in a white ocean, not knowing where to steer. It wasn't just that all my classmates were white now. It was the culture of things as well. I had to adapt to it. It was a different reaction and awareness to everything. It would take time, I told myself.

My saving grace was Kristen. She was my lighthouse on the daily now. We had grown close over the last couple of months and I knew she was my best friend in this new world I was in. I opened my eyes and stared at the picture of her and I that we took one night together at a sleepover at her house. That was a first for me. First time I had spent the night anywhere, much less at a white person's house. Momma didn't even know I was gone. I had found her the next Saturday morning when I came home to her passed out on our bathroom floor. It was fun being at Kristen's house though that Friday night. Just being away from all of that with Momma if but for a night. Of course, it was hell to pay when I did get back to face Momma in the morning. Kristen had a great way of making me feel at ease. She saw past the color difference in it all. She was brave. She was real. She was confident and even more confident in the areas I was not. The boys in our grade and above loved Kristen and that confidence. I love to see her interact with them, always leaving them wanting more and not ever taking them too seriously. She guarded her heart, and that was something I always grew up learning how to do, so we were alike in that way. I guess having said all that, tomorrow night would be the night I would be taken and Kristen is who I would blame.

Still facing my locker and staring at our picture, an arm came over my shoulder from behind me, slamming my locker shut. I turned to see Kristen giggling at me. She quickly came alongside me and opened my locker, gazing at our photo as I was.

"My, my, my…who is that lavish, beautiful young girl?" Kristen said playfully in some god-awful accent. We both laughed, and I closed my locker again after grabbing my books and faced Kristen. "Kristen, you study for our biology test?" I asked.

"Who needs to study when I have you with all the answers," Kristen said sarcastically.

"Oh no, Ma'am. We ain't gonna be having you cheat off me again. That got us almost kicked off the team," I said, laughing. Kristen rolled her eyes playfully, "I know. Mr. Harper is expecting me to cheat again anyways. It would be a slow death to choose that route."

Suddenly two of our boy classmates came up behind Kristen, tickling her. She laughed and turned around, slapping both of them on the shoulders. It was Danny Woods and James Giddings. Both of whom I didn't like. I could tell their intent with any girl in our school was not a genuine one. Danny had dated Kristen on and off through middle and high school, and he was her first kiss. Danny had taken Kristen's virginity two months ago and was always on a quest to do it again with her. I looked over to see while Danny and Kristen flirted, James staring me up and down sizing me up. I felt violated just by the look he had on his face. James was no good. Kristen was beginning to think so as well. Kristen had grown up with him, and she had that trust with him, but I was having trouble. James was a heavy partier, and the rumors through the halls where he had slept with girls two years older than him as well as girls two years younger still in middle school. But the way he was looking at me, I could tell he wanted to take something of mine as well.

"So Brittany, you and your accomplice here free tomorrow night? 'Hot Tub Time Machine' is playing at The Palace downtown, and we are all going," James said.

"Who is 'we,' James," I asked.

Kristen and Danny turned now, giving their attention to our conversation. "Yeah, Brit, I thought it'd be fun. Are you free tomorrow night? You can stay at my house if you like," Kristen replied.

"Yeah, and you guys can ride with us to Ben's party afterward if you like," James said, chiming in.

James was known as the car guy around the school. Girls and his 1970 prime condition Buick Skylark was his identity. Not grades or sports. It was his car and conquering girls. I looked to see all three looking at me for an immediate answer as though I was the missing wheel for this double date being set in motion right in front of me. With perfect timing, the bell rang, and I told them I'd think about it.

"Please do," James replied to me as he glided past, heading to his next class. The school was his kingdom. So he thought anyway in his own little world. I always wondered how my life would have gone if I had gotten in his car that night. It no doubt would have been different. I didn't, though. I never made it into the backseat of James's Buick Skylark. I was destined for darker waters.

Chapter 11
Cal Sullivan

The gun blast rattled the walls and sat me straight up in bed on alert. I looked over at my clock on the nightstand. It was 3:30 in the morning. I had dreaded the worst. The blast sounded like it had gone off right by my head. It had been a month now since my momma had pulled that shotgun on Poppa and he had fled off into the night. Poppa had eventually come back in two days' time. Momma had stayed in her bedroom the entire time crying on and off by her lonesome. When Poppa did show, he said not a word but went to his basement and stayed there for the next couple days. Eventually, after another week, we were back to normal as normal could be in our circumstances. It would be just Momma and I with Poppa gone doing Lord knows what. However, these past few days I had noticed Momma had reached a breaking point. There was a weight sinking on her but I could never place it. It was guilt in fact. Didn't know what for though? For Poppa beating us? She would argue and be beaten by Poppa nightly for the past several nights in a row now. I guess Poppa had reached his breaking point too this night. They had fought on and off all night after supper. I sat and listened to things breaking all around the house as I lay there quietly under my covers trying to block it out.

Moments had passed now and I finally got the courage to go inspect. I slid the covers off of me and placed my feet to the cold floor slowly. I started to catch the subtle smell of gun smoke. It was that unique smell of gunpowder sulfur that is unmistakable. As I crept towards my door, I could hear my poppa yelling gibberish under his breath and cursing while stumbling around in the kitchen. He'd been drinking sure enough. I then heard him open the back kitchen door and stagger out. I opened my bedroom door slowly and crept along our short little hallway towards the kitchen and stopped at the doorway to my parents' bedroom. I could see my momma's little toes sticking out from the other end of the bed. They were lifeless. My eyes burned a little bit from the gun smoke that had gathered and was lifting to the ceiling. I stared at her feet there for a good minute, lost. I knew Poppa had taken her. She had fought him all she could but Poppa had had enough. He'd found that shotgun Momma hid from him. Either that or Momma aimed to kill Poppa herself with that gun tonight and he then took it from her hands. I turned and looked out at the end of the hall past the kitchen to the darkness beyond the outside of the back kitchen door as it sat wide open on its hinges rocking from the wind. That is all I could hear now was the strong late winter gusts hitting the house. I could hear Poppa's gibberish faintly as he was yelling to himself outside in that darkness. A minute or so past then. BOOM! I saw the muzzle flash that lit up that darkness but for a moment like a flicker. Then it was quiet again. The gun blast still echoed through the outside into the distance like thunder. Now all but for the wind and a few startled neighborhood dogs was all I heard.

I crept again down the hallway, my body shaking. I was shell shocked to say the least. I knew in my gut what both gun blasts had been and their purpose. It took two shotgun shells to make me an orphan. I stepped to the entrance of the back door and looked out. The moon was not there tonight and all I could see were the front porch lights of our neighbors across the open lot field next to our house. I stepped out onto the back little porch stoop and thought of what to do. I didn't want to go call the police as I didn't want to step another foot in there with Momma laying there. I wept for a few minutes as the shock began to wear off a bit and some reality set in. I stepped off the back stoop and started across the field at a trot towards our neighbor's front porch lights. They would take me in and keep me warm. They could make the call to the police that I didn't want to make.

I ran fifty yards from the house and then toppled over on my face. It had been so dark I had tripped over Poppa. I looked down and could make out the black silhouette of my dad's lifeless body lying there in the tall grass. The rifle lay at his feet. I was thankful there had been no moon tonight to see much else. I knew he was dead though. I looked up at the neighbor's house that I was about to wake up and start their day unannounced. It was going to be a long night for the Rogers family once I knocked on that door.

I sat in the back of the cop car rubbing my eyes on the blanket the Rogers had given me to keep myself warm. I already missed Momma, something terrible. There were now dozens of cop cars lined up and down the street like a parade. The flashing blue and red lights flooded the neighborhood now and made my eyes blurry. I watched as the red and blue beams danced off the side of our little old white house tucked back on our open block. I thought best to just keep my eyes shut. I sat alone in silence while deputy Dekins was out preparing to take me to the station to make a statement.

Whatever that meant. I opened my eyes and looked across to see the dark black body bags that my folks were zipped up in. They were loaded into the back of the sheriff van and I watched them get hauled away down the street. I guess I thought in the end my poppa would have it coming to him but why did God take Momma too because of my poppa's own doings? I looked over further out the window and noticed for the first time since Christmas our old church steeple lit up cresting over the trees. It was then I got the urge to pray. I haven't prayed since Poppa hit me for the first time and that was years ago. I thought on praying at Christmas but we never made it to the service that night when Momma pulled that shotgun. Momma and I didn't pray on that sidewalk bench that night either. I guess you don't have to be in church to talk to the good Lord though. I knew that. What was the use? Seeing my parents hauled off in body bags made it pointless now. I guess God was pointless. He sure didn't care about the family in that house out the cop car window.

It must have been several minutes later for I am not sure how long I was asleep. I must have nodded off contemplating on praying and found myself still slumped over in the back of the deputy car with my new blanket. I rubbed my eyes and looked out the window once again on my side to see the red and blues still flashing widely and there seemed to be even more cars now and a news crew. It had gotten crowded while I was sleeping. Seconds later deputy Dekins hopped in the driver seat shutting his door. He turned back to ask how I was doing. I was able to stumble out a few syllables. "I'm good," I stuttered. He then reluctantly turned back and put the car in drive and we started to cruise in front of my house that was now crawling with police and people in suits like ants on a dirt mound.

"I am glad you made it out son," Dekins muttered. "Turns out that was a bad place in that there house you were livin' in, boy," he said.

As we cruised slowly by my front porch, I looked to see a couple of guys in badges and suits carrying two young blond little girls in blankets out of the front door. They looked around eleven or twelve. Just a little older than me but I didn't know them just by looking at them at a glance. They were crying and they were dirty. It looked like they had been through a whole hell of a lot too. More than me I reckon. I would find out later they were my poppa's treasures he kept in our basement.

Chapter 12
Brittany Johnson

The coolness of our refrigerator freezer felt good on my hot face. I was fuming. I dug into the back of the freezer and popped a few ice cubes from the tray and wrapped a paper towel around them, putting the ice against my cheek. I leaned against the freezer opening and then got a hold of myself. I was cooling off both inside and out.

Momma was liquored up early tonight and when we got into it, she started swinging.

It was my sophomore year and it had been a big month. I turned 15, I had been reassigned to a different high school, and was playing basketball with all white girls now except for Beatrice who transferred with me. The story claimed in the local newspaper that our high school on the south side was getting condemned. Shut down. Apparently south Texas humidity and floods don't do school buildings too well. It increases Father Time by two-fold, they say down here. They had tried for ten years to pass a community school bond to build us a new high school as ours was over sixty years old. That times the floods and humidity made our school well past due to do so. Problem faced was getting everyone to indeed vote for the color kids on the south side. The bond never came and we were shut down and dispersed. Now all the color kids on the south side were everyone's problem in Gilbertson. God, I knew had a sense of humor about things from above.

There have been a lot of changes. There were a lot of changes and a lot of white people I had to acclimate to. All that mixed with puberty going on and my momma's daily habits had me a bit on edge to say the least. Momma was now on another job, her third in the past four months. The drinking had gotten worse in the last couple of years and it started to pour into the day now. Momma would barely speak to me now or look me in the eye these days because she knew. She knew. She knew how I felt. The whole damn apartment smelled of guilt, shame, and vodka. I couldn't stand it and tonight was where my pot boiled over with my momma. It was my starting game on the new team and on top of that it was parents' night. I had been nervous about Momma in her state walking out on that gym floor in front of a crowd with her. Then I having to put on a smile while holding hands and posing for pictures. In the end, I wanted her there though.

Momma and I had been building towards tonight. We had made a pact even. I would score twenty points in the game if she promised to stay sober for the night and walk me across the gym floor for the ceremony. We shook on it. We hugged on it. In fact, at that moment it was indeed the first time we had made eye contact with each other in months. It felt good to make that connection and in that exact moment I felt the truth from her. She had promised me. Broken promises from Momma were constant but in that moment it felt different. I also thought it was good she had a short-term goal to strive for if it wasn't me on the daily. I mean wasn't that what rehab was all about.

Goals? My pappy and mama had tried and tried to put her in a program for her drugs and alcohol but her stubbornness always won in the end every time. She always kept some kind of job I did have to give her that. She even didn't drink last night to top it off so we were on the right track for a good night. Things were looking up. However, come today it all came to a crash.

I had gotten home from school early to chill and get ready for the game. My mom had done the same and had gotten off even earlier from her job. She came home to an empty apartment with nothing to do and me not there. For an addict that was dynamite. Momma had given in in only thirty minutes and walked herself over to our corner liquor store three blocks away and bought her that vodka bottle. When I came home an hour later, I found her collapsed on the floor rolling around. I opened the door and she started laughing at me. That is when I lost it. I was done. I snapped. I snatched the vodka bottle from the kitchen counter top and chunked it over her head. The bottle shattered glass all into my mom's hair when it hit the wall above her. My mother slowly turned up to look at me. Her eyes were scolding hot.

"Brittany J, you better watch yourself girl," Momma said in a low tone. "Ain't no need for that. What the hell is a matter with you?" she asked.

I couldn't even see straight. I was so upset at her. Without thinking I charged her, tackling her to the ground. We began rolling on the ground pulling hair and going off on each other. She got on top of me at one point throwing fists to my face while cursing me. At one point, she over swung and I was able to flip her off me. She stood up but lost her balance and fell over the end table taking out our only living room lamp. Momma then stood up over me wincing. Her arm started to bleed. She had at one point rolled into some of the glass from the vodka bottle that I shattered and it had cut her deep.

The pain sobered her up and we stood in silence as she leaned over the kitchen sink while letting me dress her wound and bandage it with whatever we had in our apartment. She didn't dare look at me the whole time I bandaged her. Just before she closed her bedroom door in my face to go to bed she turned to me.

"I can't wait until you outta here and can leave me alone."

She then shut the door in my face and I sank to the floor in tears. I kept quiet though. I didn't want to give any satisfaction to her that it had fazed me but of course it did.

I sat alone on my front porch apartment stoop for a long time crying. I missed daddy. I wondered what he was doing now. Where was he? Did he go to heaven?

Daddy did always have a strong faith. He got us up every Sunday morning, if he hadn't worked too hard the day before, and made Momma and I dress up to go sweat sitting in our little white church by the river praising Jesus. It was daddy that prayed at our meals and at dinner always giving thanks. He for sure was a Christian. He was baptized as well in the same river I was and the same church decades ago. I felt he had led a life of faith up until the end. Right before that train came that one night to take him though he had at the time strayed away. Momma and him were fighting a lot over bills and me. I had noticed too that he and Momma had turned away from each other in the end. They focused on their jobs, friends, and themselves alone and not each other. I could tell it was a weight on daddy's shoulders by doing that. It was that weight that led him to drugs and drinking. Then that one night that train did come.

The ice had completely melted and the side of my face was numb from the homemade ice pack I had made for myself. Momma had really connected one on my jaw. I had been waiting on pappy for twenty minutes now to come scoop me up and take me to my game. He came to every one. I was thankful for him and mama. I am glad they were still in my life. I often thought about going and living with them but I knew that would very well cut the cord and maybe even end my momma's life if she was left alone here to herself knowing I had up and left her. More minutes passed and I began to get worried but sure enough I heard in the distance pappy's old tan and rusted Cadillac clunker making its way down our street slowly. Pappy pulled up to the front curb with a trail of exhaust smoke trailing behind him like a cloud of death. I got up and made my way and got in the passenger seat.

"Mama ain't comin'?" I asked.

"She got to finish makin' somethin' at the house she wanted to give ya and we will go by and get her. Then go," pappy said smiling.

His smile stopped short when he noticed the whelp on the side of my face from Momma. "Goodness now, what happened there?" he asked.

"What do you think happened pappy?" I asked back in a knowing tone.

Pappy sunk down and lowered his head, closing his eyes. He knew it had happened again. It had become all too common. "She struck you again eh, Brit," Pappy asked defeated. I nodded to him.

"I knew when you called earlier to come and getcha. I knew it just by the tone in your voice she had done that to ya again…my word," he said.

Pappy opened his eyes again and looked up at me. "You alright baby girl?"

I nodded but I couldn't hold back this time like I had done many times before.

Tears were already streaming down my face and I broke. Pappy then took me and held me in his arms for a while as I cried and ruined his shirt in the process from my water works. He just held me and that's all I needed. We sat there on the street curb in silence for a few minutes then just staring at the apartment window where we knew Momma was passed out inside.

"You know she loves you very much," pappy said. "Yeah…but she loves herself more," I replied.

Pappy was silent at that response. A moment passed again and pappy took my hand and held it tight.

"Brittany J, I pray for her every night. I pray that the good Lord will reveal himself to her. That he will knock herself upside the head with his presence and that she will have clarity and see all that she has in front of her. I pray that prayer every night Brittany J," Pappy said, squeezing my hand. "You need to be praying that every night too if you ain't," he said.

Thinking about it, I haven't prayed since daddy died. I had kind of gone numb with God after that. I just couldn't see why if God was so perfect, so powerful, and so filled with love and peace for us that he then let daddy get killed on a train track or Momma to get to the state she is now and beating her daughter? Why?

"Pappy, why should I pray?" I asked flat out. Pappy then looked up at me. "Why should I pray? What good is it? Why does God let these things happen to me? Why does God let Daddy die and Momma become a drunk? Why should I pray to him, uh?!" I said, pleading.

Pappy took a beat and locked eyes with me delicately stroking the side of my face that had swollen. "Brittany J, God made you. He made you in his image and he does love you. These things happen to your folks because there is what we know as sin on this earth. And when we turn to sin and don't choose to follow Him than we become lost Brittany J. We become lost and the result can be death. Death and loss and suffering is all a means to soften the heart and turn us back to the Lord….to then follow him now," he said.

Pappy then took a moment and wrapped his arm around me.

"That is what you need to do now Britt. Follow him once again. Submit to him and he will lead you," pappy said.

"God's not here," I said staring out the car window off into the distance at our run-down apartment complex.

"Awwww, but he is. He is all around us. He gotta hand in this conversation we havin' too whether you like it or not," he said.

I looked up at him. We both had tears in our eyes and we hugged. God bless pappy. I started to think right then and there maybe God did if anything place pappy now in my life as my rock. I was almost certain of it now. I never did pray to God until after I was abducted and everything was stripped from me but God himself. It would be a little over three months from now. No, I didn't pray that afternoon in that car for Momma but it was at that moment with my pappy that I started thinking of God again. He wasn't as distant now and that was a good thing. I am going to need Him.

Chapter 13
Cal Sullivan

I laid dripping in sweat staring at the ceiling and listening to the hum of the air condition units on the roof doing their mediocre job of cooling the place. The sounds of my fellow roommates snoring made me agitated and wore me down night after night now. After that fateful day that I saw my folks zipped up in bags and then I myself was ridden away in deputy Deakins car from my folks' house, I had gone through some ups and downs to say the least. My parents' death was ruled a homicide with the fault going to my poppa as the murderer of my momma. He then took his life there as well. That's all no surprise. What was a surprise is that I actually stayed with deputy Deakins and his nice family for a week until my only next of kin on either side, uncle Bobby, my momma's younger brother, came to claim me out of pure pressure, obligation, and mostly opportunity for himself.

That first week though with the deputy's family sure was good. We ate good every night and they had two young boys that were just a little older than me that took me right in as their own. I got to sleep in their bunk beds and the deputy's wife reminded me of Momma before my brother died and dad had sunk his teeth into her. She was sweet and doted on the whole family. It was a nice change and some of those days in that week I actually went without thinking of what happened or of Momma or Poppa for that matter. I was caught up in being in a normal family.

At the end of that week, we buried my folks out in the southeast cemetery of Gilbertson. The poor man's cemetery was what it was known for. Not much to look at and I could tell maintenance and upkeep wasn't a priority. Poppa didn't even have plots purchased so they were buried technically outside the cemetery by a ditch on the backside of the property. Uncle Bobby came down from North Texas and attended the funeral with me and the deputy's family. That was all the people there for the ceremony. Given that even though Poppa did shoot Momma, we had the funeral together as a joint ceremony. To save time and money, I guess. I thought it was pretty weird myself but I didn't holler about it.

After we all watched in silence, the gravedigger put the last crumb of dirt on my parents two graves and then Uncle Bobby, a short and squat heavy man that would profusely sweat and had fidgety eyes, wiped his brow and asked the deputy for my suitcase that was already packed and waiting in Deakins car. Momma always said Uncle Bobby had a good heart down deep but had trouble landing on the right side of the law on things most of the time. I could tell just being close to Deakins in uniform made my uncle uneasy. I walked over and hugged Deakins' family. It had only been a week but we all cried. I think that made uncle Bobby even more uneasy. I didn't want to go. I liked where I was now and thought I had a good family now but I always knew deep down it was not my own. Now the obese man that held my suitcase wearing a white and heavily stained seersucker suit was all I had left. I got in his beat up old Chevelle and we drove back to my folk's house. Uncle Bobby being the only next to kin on both sides, got me and the house together. I think he really was only wanting the latter but was stuck with both. From what Momma told me, I was figuring this house was a relief to him financially or just a place to finally have a stable roof under his head that he would probably sell eventually.

We pulled up in front of my old white house and I got a queasy feeling in the pit of my stomach. All the memories came flooding back. I was hoping to never see his place again. We later ate in silence that night at the same table Momma and I would sit at and have our talks and eat our TV dinners. I watched as my uncle Bobby devoured his own TV dinner like a lion on a gazelle.

"We gonna be fine boy. We gonna get cha back in school and get things back to normal," uncle Bobby said, spraying food out of his mouth that landed on his chin and then his shirt.

"Then I will get workin' on gettin' things set up here," he said.

I had no idea what that meant but I nodded and continued to push food around on my TV dinner tray. Later that night, I snuck out of my bed. Given the circumstances I felt suffocated in my own home. Only this wasn't my home now. It never would be. Uncle Bobby seems to forget that the room he now slept in was the room I saw my momma laying there after Poppa took her. I stared at the door to my parents' room that was shut. I thought of Momma laying there that one night as I listened to uncle Bobby sawing logs through the door. The whole house seemed to shake. I stepped out quietly through the back kitchen door onto the short back porch stoop and listened to the lazy early summer crickets. They were humming and luckily had drowned out my uncle's breathing from inside. Minutes later I found myself walking past the open lot next to our house and threw the grove of trees out back where the creek lay that took my brother so long ago. I sat on a boulder on the bank in the moonlight staring at the water moving under my feet and thought about my brother. What he looked like when he died and how Momma must have looked when she found him and was whaling those noises that I heard that made it all the way back to our house that day. My brother always was the believer of the family. Momma said despite his craftiness he had the heart that followed Jesus. I was too young to know. Apparently, Momma figured he would be a preacher man one day. She said my brother knew what it was like to show grace as God did to us. I hope he is there now in heaven with God. It was a nice thought. But how could there be a God that would let all this happen. Ain't no way he exists. I bent down at my feet and picked up a bright yellow torn wrapper of some sort that I would never know in the darkness that night what it actually was. What I held in my hand was actually a worn shredded piece of police caution tape from my brother's death scene marking off his body that once had laid here. It had survived the elements all these years. I crumbled up the piece of trash in my hand and sent it on downstream. I stood then looking up at the moon and walked back to that house that was once my home.

We went on living together in my old house for another six months. When I say "we" I mean me, myself, and I as I never saw uncle Bobby after the second week we got there. Uncle Bobby kept the freezer stocked for me and would come home drunk a few nights a week at five in the morning. The rest of the week he'd be gone all together leaving me alone in that house to myself. Finally, after those six months deputy Deakins showed up to take me away again. I would go to live with him and his family for a few weeks. I found out later that Uncle Bobby fell again on the wrong side of the law and was running an underground card game and casino in an abandoned warehouse not too far away from the house that got tipped off. Hard to keep something like that quiet in a town like Gilbertson. Uncle Bobby went back to jail and I got to go back to my new family once again. However, it wouldn't last. Deakins and his family told me they loved me but couldn't keep me. Two months later, we drove to the state foster home six miles outside Bay City, Texas just south of Houston and dropped me off. We once again hugged, cried, and just like that I watched their family station wagon drive away from me back down the long dirt road. I was alone again.

I rolled over on my side and then back on my back again letting out a huge sigh of frustration. The beds in this state foster home were less than to be desired. It felt like I was laying on a pile of gravel. I glanced over and noticed the crucifix that was nailed to the wall above my head. I had long nights like this one where I would lay awake and just stare at it. Wondering. I would wonder where God was in all of this? Why had he taken Momma away from me? Why couldn't it be simple and I just had lived with Deakins and his family? It was a simple happy ending but the fact was God wasn't there. At least not for me.

I had been in the foster home a year and half. I am twelve years old now with a birthday around the corner. With each passing week in this place, I grow angrier. I grow angrier towards everyone and everything and how my cards were dealt. Staring every night up at that cross above my head didn't help any. That cross was gasoline on my fire. I had tried a few times to rip it from off that wall but unlike the air conditioning and my bed, they had done a good job of keeping it intact. The cross was supposed to be a comfort. It was supposed to be a symbol of hope in our situation of loss and uncertainty as an orphan. I found no such meaning. All I found was someone who let me down. To add to my anger and misery, I had been abused a few times since my stay here outside of Bay City. Once by the older foster child who I housed with that slept three bunks down from me just because I looked at him wrong one day. He would find me in the shower a handful of times and give me new pairs of black eyes. Then there was Donnie, the janitor here, who would drag me into the cleaning supply closet on off hours of the night occasionally to take advantage and put some beatings on me when I had it in me to try and fight him off. I was broken now and nothing filled or fueled me but the anger. That crucifix above me burnt my eyes to look at it while I laid there.

I must have finally nodded off and went into a deep sleep. It was heavy. I began dreaming and saw images once again of my old white house. It was dusk and it was snowing out with six or eight inches on the ground blanketing everything white that I saw. I myself was standing looking at my house lit up from inside from across the open lot field that separated us. I began running towards the lights of my house smiling and knowing that Momma was there waiting for me. As I ran though, I began to get tired and breathing became hard for me as the snow got deeper. Before I knew it, I had tripped over an object covered by the snowfall, sending me into a snow faceplant on the ground. I raised my head and wiped snow from my eyes to see my poppa's snow-covered body lying there camouflaged in white. He was in the same position that he laid the night I found him in the field out beside our house in the dark. There was no blood anywhere to be found. I timidly reached my hand out and wiped snow away from his covered face to reveal Poppa with an evil unsettling grin that never wavered.

He seemed to be staring right through me like he would come alive any second.

I quickly stood up and kept running through the snow that had significantly gotten deeper on me since I fell over Poppa. The snow line was hitting my thighs as I trudged through the snowfall. It hurt to breathe and I became very tired. I winced in pain and exhaustion but pushed myself to reach the back door. By this time the snow fell so heavy and thick I could barely see a few feet past me. I opened up my back door and stepped inside collapsing to the ground to catch my breath. I was immediately warm though and the kitchen smelled of Momma and her cooking back when my brother was alive. I sat up thinking I heard something. In the stillness and the snow falling outside the windows, I could hear Momma's voice faintly. She was calling me. "Cal baby. Come here. I need you. Come here my baby," she called.

I rose and made my way down the hall. Momma's voice was getting louder. I got beside the door leading to Poppa's basement. Momma was down there. I opened the basement door and began to inch my way down the stairs. My mother's voice called louder as she called for me. I got towards the bottom of the basement staircase to see Momma sitting on the basement floor in her classic nightgown and her hair all done up nicely. She was clutching and hoovering over the two little blond girls I saw that day on my front porch in blankets when I was taken away by the deputies. They were dirty and tired looking like before but happy to be in my momma's embrace who seemed to be giving them new clothes to wear. Mother smiled at me and I smiled back in relief to see her happy. Suddenly, her smile drained away and I saw panic in her eyes. I then felt a large hand of claws touch my shoulder making its way to my throat. My mother began to scream.

Then…I sat up in bed suddenly shouting to myself. My cot was soaked now in sweat. I rubbed the sweat away from my eyes and worked to catch my breath. I looked around the room to see my screaming had not awoken my fifteen other roommates that lay scattered around me in the foster home. I sat in silence catching my breath and taking in the stillness after such a dream I just had. That is when I heard her again. Was it her? I held my breath now and strained to hear as though my ears were playing tricks on me. However, I swear I heard what I heard. It was Momma's voice. She was calling for me. She was here. She was here at the foster home. She was saying the same words from my dream, "Cal. Cal baby. I need you." Her voice was so faint but so rich as though it was piercing right through my very soul. After several minutes, I still heard it laying there in my cot but tried to ignore the sounds and put my pillow over my face.

Enough is enough. I flung my covers away and sat my feet on the cold old linoleum floor and made my way past all the snores. I poked my head out looking down the long dark hallway. Momma's voice was now a little louder. Richer. A little more clear. It was intoxicating. I tiptoed down the hallway in my pj's with my head on a damn swivel. If I were caught, it'd be hell to pay in labor with possible beatings to go with it. I couldn't stop myself though. Momma's voice was magnetic and I was sure she was just beyond every door that I went through. Finally, after making my journey through many doors and stair wells, I came to the old metal door labeled "caution." It was the door that led down to the boiler room. I pushed the door open with a few hard shoulder strikes and opened it to a long dark staircase in front of me leading downward. I could then hear the immediate humming of the boilers below. However, my mother's voice was piercing now and it tugged at my chest. "Cal. I am right down here, Cal. Come to me, baby." She sounded as though she was just there at the bottom of the stairs beyond the pool of dark. She sounded so comforting. I longed to hug her. She was here I am certain.

I pressed forward and when I got to the bottom of the stairs, I called Momma but no answer. It was then that I felt its presence for the first time. It was that of bottomless fear. A fear I had never felt before. I tried to lift my head to look in the corner of the room where the back boiler sat but couldn't due to my shear trembling. I wet the floor beneath me at my feet and before I knew it, I was cast towards the brick wall and bounced off flopping to the ground. I cried out in pain from my back. It was then my body was paralyzed and I couldn't move. I felt the presence then hover directly over me now as I lay on my back breathing heavily. My head was turned to the side and I wanted to look at what was in front of me but couldn't because of the direct physical heat. It felt like it was burning my face to try and turn to look and the thing that now stared down at me. It smelled of sulfur and the death of an animal that had been left to rot. It was then that it entered me through my chest as though razor blades had pierced through me. I wanted to scream but nothing came out. From that point on that was the last true point, I remember myself as truly my own. It was the last time I had a memory of my own self driven thought. From that point on, I was held trapped in both body and soul. I was only a vessel now being controlled by something dark that I could not run away from or do anything about. It was here now and it controlled all of me that I knew of myself. The presence began to whisper in my mind as I laid there paralyzed among the boilers on the ground. Its voice was low and calm but had an eeriness to it that was almost like a reptile and very ancient. It called itself, Abaddon.

Chapter 14
Brittany Johnson

Pushing the front lobby doors to the downtown movie theater open, the hot and muggy heat of south Texas hit like a tidal wave. Kristen and I, as planned, had gone with James Giddings and Danny Woods to the movies the following night on a double date against my own will. What wasn't planned was James and Danny skipping out on the movie half way through to go joy ride around in James' car drinking and hitting the county back roads. As they got up from their theater seats to leave, James turned to me and whispered "this movie isn't very funny. I am into action movies anyway. We will be back in an hour to come scoop y'all up." And with that they left. I was relieved. Kristen was pissed that Danny had left her. She rolled her eyes sitting in her seat and immediately got on her phone. It was 2010 and not many sophomore high schoolers had a phone and or as nice of a phone that Kristen had but she made the case that her mom got it for her to bribe her for bad parenting…and to keep tabs on her and where she went. I myself had no phone. Momma had one but pappy and mama still just used a landline. I guess my grandfolks were a little more trusting of me anyway.

We now stood outside the theater looking for our dates that had escaped.

Kristen tried Danny's cell but no answer. As we started to sweat, we made conversation with a few classmates from our school that had the same idea of coming to the movies on a Friday night. There was buzz around the social circles as we stood out on the sidewalk of a keg party at a senior's house that had graduated last year but it had already gotten busted an hour ago. That's a good thing. I wasn't much of a drinker.

Kristen made me try whiskey and gin from her parents' liquor cabinet one night when I had stayed over but it didn't agree with me. I was sick half the night with Kristen playing my nurse. I think she was just so scared we were going to get busted that she never pressured with me about alcohol after that night. I watched Kristen chat it up with our fellow students about the busted party as I stood in silence and observed. Kristen, no matter what she told you, was a popular person on campus and knew a lot of people in every grade. She had that kind of draw and personality about her.

As I stood there watching Kristen talk it up as we stood under the old marquee, I scanned around at our surroundings. The old movie theater marquee sign lit up in the darkness faintly shining on all the ole brick and mortar buildings of the old downtown. A lot of the old buildings stood vacant and abandoned like ghosts from another time. It was dead to say the least. The only activity going this evening was us out front on the sidewalk here. However, something did catch my eye. Maybe it was a movement I had noticed. Diagonally across the street alongside the old abandoned bank building in the shadows stood parked an old truck. I thought I saw a silhouette of a man sitting in the driver's seat but it was so dark I couldn't be sure. It all had a familiar vibe to it but I couldn't place it. I did suddenly have the feeling wash over me of being watched as I stood in the group of girls on the sidewalk.

We talked a little more waiting for our ride which was Danny and James but they had yet to show. Kristen's mom had dropped us off and we said we would get a ride home after the movie. Kristen wasn't concerned that her mom would stay up worrying about us either. One by one the crowd drifted away until finally fifteen minutes later we were by ourselves. Kristen tried Danny's phone one more time but it went to voicemail. Kristen shrugged and let out a shout of frustration. I was relieved to be truthful. Going back to Kristen's house sounded just my speed. We began walking down the sidewalk a few steps. Kristen started dialing to phone her mother to come get us when we heard the unmistaken rumble of James' engine turning the corner. I could hear the music blaring from his car already from two blocks away. We turned and Kristen waved, smiling, flagging them down. James' hot rod cruised up next to us on the curb and James killed the music. Danny rolled down his window. His eyes were bloodshot and he squinted to look us up and down.

"Alright, alright, alright," Danny slurred. Kirsten giggled catching the famous line quote of Matthew McConaughey which had gone right over my head.

"Where were you guys? We were going home I'll have you know," Kristen replied leaning on the car next to Danny's window. "Well good. We got here just in the nick of time then ladies," James said with a creepy smirk. He had already started to look me up and down studying my features as though he hoped to meet all I had to offer later that night. Like he was expecting it.

"Bummer about Ben's party getting busted. Have you guys heard about that already?" Danny asked.

"Yeah, we heard," Kristen replied leaning into the window giving Danny a kiss. Meanwhile, I stood back with my hand on my hips. I was ready to leave.

"Danny, you're already drunk," Kristen said giggling while stepping away from James' car. "I am not. Come on," he pleaded. "We just went for a couple of beers while you all finished the movie," James piped in.

"Yeah well, brave of y'all to be driving around with beer," Kristen said.

"Uh, no worries I am a professional," James replied, letting out a belch. "We are going home I think," Kristen said. "Sounds good to me," I said, chiming in.

"Wait, wait, wait. You ladies come out with us. It is still early!" James yelled. "Kristen, come to the bridge with us. Bring Britt and you guys come have one beer with us and we will take you home. I promise," Danny pleaded, slurring his words leaning out the car window, and grasping Kristen's hand. He pouted his big eyes at Kristen begging her. Pathetic.

"Yeah…promise," James said while burning a hole right through me and undressing me with his mind all at the same time. His eyes too were bloodshot and that of a predator on his prey. He was sweating. I reached for Kristen and pulled her to me back on the sidewalk.

"Come on Kris let's go girl. Not tonight. I just wanna bail and go back to your house," I said. I didn't have a good feeling about any of this. Kristen looked at me and then back at the boys who were egging her on. She caved.

"Let's just go have one beer and we will go. Okay? I swear," Kristen said. I stared at her for a long while pleading with my eyes but Kristen had Danny on her mind.

"Go ahead and go Kris but I am going home," I said. Kristen begged me for a few more minutes but I stood my ground. There was no way I was going to get in that car with 'All the way James' trying to touch me all the rest of the night. Kristen gave me her phone to call my grandfolks to then pick me up and like that before I could say another word James peeled out and they were gone. All I was left to now was the hum of crickets and the main highway that was droning with cars off in the distance.

I plopped down on the curb and dialed for my pappy and mama's house. Momma was either busy working or passed out already and wouldn't answer her phone. I was hurt. It was the first time I saw Kristen make that selfish of a choice. I know we were young friends but I thought we were better friends than for her to ditch me at the curb at night by myself. I was hurt. I was mad at her. I was tired. My mind began to drift as I sat in the silence. I envisioned James' car rumble around the block to Kristen coming back to get me after coming to her senses. We would then both leave James and Danny literally at the curb and walk home together laughing the night off. I was quickly jarred awake though back to my senses I heard the ignition of a car start up. I lifted my head slowly from my lap and looked up in the direction that I had seen the parked truck. I saw the soft glow of a cigarette light up and flicker in the shadows. There was someone there after all. I held my breath. Fear crept slowly over my body and tingled the back of my neck. The phone rang and rang but pappy never picked up. Odds are they were already in bed and both had pulled their Medicaid hearing aids out and were fast asleep. What I would never find out was I had only missed my mama from answering the phone and talking to her by a couple seconds. I had hung up the phone too quickly on mama to get there to answer my call.

I stood up and stared at the dark truck for a long minute. I didn't know what to do. Do I run? Do I keep calling on the phone? To who? If I scream would anyone even hear me this time of night in this ghost town? I turned the opposite way of the truck and began walking down the sidewalk. I would head towards my grandfolks place. It was only a few miles away and a lot closer than me and Momma's apartment. I glanced my head up to see out of the side of my eye that the truck had crept out onto the road and was tailing me. A lump formed in my throat and I started to cry. What was going to happen? My legs were starting to go numb but I started running out of instinct. The adrenaline kicked in and I picked up speed. I could hear the truck rev it's engine and started to gain on me. His headlights flicked on, shining then on my backside. He was closing in. Why did she leave me?

Chapter 15
Abaddon

I soared over Gilbertson at a bird's eye view early in the dawn of a Friday morning. I used this down time away from my main captive's body to do reconnaissance of my own while letting my captive's body recuperate and have pure oxygen and rest apart from me. As I mentioned before, I was at liberty to leave my captive from time to time so that I wouldn't kill him. Not quickly anyway. My main captive was a sheepish man of twenty-four named Callan Sullivan. Like I mentioned, he was the perfect long term for me. He was unassuming in appearance that allowed me to get close to my prey when need be to strike.

However, long durations of my presence within him would deteriorate his body and mind at a dramatic pace. Therefore, I would make it customary to exit his body every four or five days at a time for his body to catch up with itself; to breathe in all simple terms. But I would only stay long enough away to give his body a rest and not his mind. Just about the time he would perhaps start having consciousness again of his true surroundings and recollection of his past of when I first entered him, I would show myself again to his soul where I would stay until I let him come back up for air once again. I never wanted to be gone long enough though to risk The Creator finding a way to reach him. Not this one.

On this particular morning, the sun was rising and I had already made various circle routes above the sleeping commune checking in on my other various side projects I had going that may need recruitment. Hours earlier, I had made my way over to the north side of the city where I had been checking in on a certain young soul in the household of the Peterson family. There was a troubled youth there that was seeking my Lordship Lucifer's guidance and acceptance. This young man whom I speak of is planning a lethal attack on his school where he pursues his education. That would be extraordinary. To think of how many souls he could take and the mass damage that could cause extending well out to all over the city by the amount of loss and hatred it could bring. The young man has the drive but still lacks full confidence. This is where I have been coming into play, looming outside his window as he prays to my master. I know now after visiting him tonight he is ready. Though it will not be me to capture him or enter him for I already have my dwelling. It will have to be a fellow member that will have to travel here to enter. I have already put in a request to his Lordship to have this accomplished very soon if it's meant to be.

I hadn't always been the bottom dweller of my kind working on the front lines. Limited to just a soul here or there and taking orders if you will. Actually, there has been mass confusion as to who I am and exactly my role in the scheme of it all. Some who know me by name say I am Lucifer, his Lordship himself. Some think I am still an angel of God still doing The Creator's bidding for destruction in his name. The truth is I am Abaddon, the fallen angel of Lucifer. I am one from the original realm that left the Creator and followed his Lordship below in the beginning of our kind. I was one of the original castaways. Why at one point after we were set in our permanent home below, I was fourth in overall ranking to his Lordship, Lucifer when we descended. However, I fell. Yes, even a fallen angel can fall twice I am afraid. I became selfish. I started to recruit the other fallen as my own to then break away and when his Lordship got wind of this I was banished. Demoted if you will. First it was to the pit of lost souls deep below. My job was to stir the fire pits and cauldrons below that the lost souls entered. This was one of the lowest of the low. The heat, putrid smell, and noise of the lost souls screams and torments could haunt anybody. Even a demon. All hours by myself and another rebellious soldier to the rank. We would spend all day breaking our backs and scarring our wings as we pulled the chained masses of lost souls into the fire pits below to be burned for eternity. Their screams and pleadings slowly faded to have any sort of remorse on me. Over time I began to hate all being for having to stay there in that place. Not only the Creator but his Lordship himself for putting me there. I did nothing that atrocious to deserve serving there in the pit of the eternal fire. Thankfully, not but a short while later I was transferred.

After I showed trust and integrity again, I was then promoted to the next realm where I am now, a keeper of souls here on earth. I am a soldier really in the middle ground. One day, I hope that my Lordship will once again see my efforts and loyalty to then join the throneship next to his royal darkness once again. There I can rest. There I can be still. Only drawback to that is that it is there on the throne next to my Lordship that you have all the time to think of your end when we will all be cast away into the fiery lake that will consume us. We all know it will come one day. My Lordship doesn't like to speak much on that though. Our fate of the fallen that is.

When I wasn't visiting young man Peterson at his household, I would soar to other places around Gilbertson to check on accounts. People in affairs, people consumed by drugs or alcohol, and especially those of leadership in church bodies of The Creator. If or when we were to capture one of them, that would be some of the greatest damage against our true enemy, he The Creator. I made sure that my captive always made it his priority to linger there amongst church congregations and their structures. If there was any way to penetrate those church bodies, I wanted to be ready. As I flew over downtown that was dark and half abandoned, I saw the lonely movie theater standing in its brilliance amongst all the other tired and old buildings. I wouldn't know it now, but it would be tomorrow night that my captive and I would come into such brilliant fortune and take the body of a young girl there in front of that very theater. She would become the source of great fuel and nourishment to me for years forward.

The sun began rising steadily now and I decided to make my way back to my main dwelling, Mr. Callan Sullivan. As I flew south, I could smell him. My captive was close. Flying then over a grove of large oak trees along a stretched alleyway I spotted his small truck. My captive, Callan, was sprawled out in the back truck bed, passed out. He had taken to the drink overnight no doubt which is often the case with him these days. My captive as of late has indeed been overcome with such confusion, fear, and depression by my souring presence that a bottle is usually his mediation. I lowered my wings and sat my talons down on the roof of my captive's truck and peered down at him. He was face up, drooling, with his eyes half shut. What a pathetic little one. To have a life of not knowing. To be simply a void in one's own head and a vehicle for my own efforts. I wonder how much longer he would last before his body gave out. It would be within the coming years, I'm sure. Then I would have to find a new home.

Thankfully it shouldn't be too hard as I have the prospects lining up. I quickly dove and entered him through his chest resuscitating him once again.

My captive suddenly opened his eyes, sitting up and gasping for air. He then let out a series of coughs which led to finally vomiting over the side of his truck bed. Aw, I am back again. I am at home now. My captive pushed away a pile of beer cans scattered across his truck bed tripping over his lawn equipment in the same process. He found his feet in the grass again, making himself stable on his own two legs. Callan, stood wiping his brow and remaining vomit away from his mouth with his handkerchief. He then made his way over to his truck and started it up. He knew now where he was. He knew his purpose now and was fulfilled again. We were back online.

Putting the truck in drive, my captive and I peeled away heading towards the Gilbertson Northside Methodist Church. As mentioned, I always aimed towards staying on the outskirts of 'The Creator' congregations looking for that perfect opportunity. My captive and I had found a niche with the local churches here and offering our lawn services. It was the perfect way in. We could get close to a congregation but not be overly obtrusive to risk revealing oneself. Through our work we could study the actual structures themselves as well as over time get a good look and feel for the church body, eyeing it for weakness where we could sneak in like a serpent into the baby's crib. My captive had been mowing the grass here for a few years now in which we have gathered much intel. We aim to strike the heart of it too with me sending his Lordship's recruits where need be when the proper time comes. It would be soon.

My captive and I entered the Methodist's church back parking lot and parked the truck in the same spot we had for years under the large oak for shade while unloading the lawn gear. We had hit the perfect mark for timing today as we looked out and saw that we would have a great front row view of the Methodist church preschool children playing on their play sets as we worked the yard. I love to sit and watch them as my captive works his equipment. I could day dream and see all the children playing and practicing for later life. I couldn't help but think and hope that one day with our Lordship's help, all of these young ones would be lost souls to join the masses that we could take below with us; that we could take from The Creator.

Chapter 16
Kristen Brooks

I sat and nursed my beer that Danny had given me and fanned the Texas heat away with my graduation program I discovered earlier. It was still in my dress pocket. Danny and I found ourselves randomly sitting outside on the curb of the old movie theater that Brittany had last been seen that night two years ago. I was a senior now in high school and it was graduation night. Yes, I was saying goodbye to the little city of Gilbertson and heading north to Austin to go to the university there to study marketing and advertising.

I was ready. For two years now, I had lived with the guilt of Britt's disappearance. People, including Danny, had tried to convince me otherwise but I knew I had left her. I knew it was because of me that she was gone. I left her vulnerable. Britt was keen on sports and getting a scholarship with basketball to go to college. She loved her grandparents and had big dreams. She simply didn't just up and run away somewhere. Something bad had happened to her and it left me rotting inside.

Senior year was supposed to be my highlight year and year of excitement but I have to admit, the guilt of losing my friend overshadowed it. Now I just wanted to get as far away from here as I possibly could. Going to college then was the next natural step to accomplish that. It was by accident though that Danny and I ended back up here at the scene of the crime. We both had walked the stage not four hours ago with my parents not in the stands of course Dad had qualified for 'presidents club' this year at his corporate office for hitting his sales goal numbers and was awarded a high-end trip to some exotic place. They chose the trip and made sure Ross knew what he was doing when recording on video the ceremony for my parents to watch me walk across the stage when they got back. The disconnection had gotten even worse with my parents these past few years after Britt vanished. I found myself pending much time in my room or with Danny. Mom and dad were like distant roommates now and that was all.

Danny and I had both skipped project graduation tonight for the graduating seniors. It was a chaperoned function for the whole class to make sure we weren't celebrating too hard for that particular evening. Danny wanted to go but I wasn't in the mood to celebrate. Not in that way anyhow. I wanted to go to this house party that an upcoming junior class man in our school was throwing so we went there instead. We weren't there but maybe an hour before the house was packed and the party got busted. Amongst the commotion of heading out the door I was able to grab two beers on the way out and find Danny at his truck way down the dirt road ready to peel out of there. Many of my fellow student party goers immediately went to their phones to connect on where the next party was. Surely the night wasn't over. The old movie theater downtown happened to be only a mile away so Danny pulled over to kill time and assess what the plan and or next party spot was going to be.

We sat quietly drinking our beers. Time had gotten away from us and it was now almost 5 am and the old small downtown was dark and dead. We sipped on our beers and listened to the crickets and the humming of the cars on the highway in the far distance. Images of Brittany's face that night as I shut the door to James' car and rolled away leaving Britt flooded my mind. We were sitting in the exact spot I had left here. I laid my head on Danny's shoulder and drank more in silence. It was here in Danny's nook I felt safe. I felt needed. I felt some shelter from pain and guilt and fear. Danny and I had been on and off all of our middle and high school careers but became official our senior year. He had taken my virginity in ninth grade and I felt attached to him because of that commitment ever since.

However, Danny Woods had changed in the past year. He was more reserved now and didn't want to party as much. Last summer he had gone to a church camp with a cousin and said he had found God and was a believer or whatever now. I wasn't sure what all that meant but he said he had a relationship now with Jesus. All it meant to me was that we didn't have sex anymore. It sucked but there wasn't anyone else in our school I wanted to be with so I had to roll with it.

Danny had tried to get me to go to church with him these last few months but I didn't. I didn't want to. I was mad at God if there was one. How could he let things happen in my life come to pass as they did with parents that couldn't be bothered and a best friend that went missing? How could God allow that to happen if he was who he said he was? Danny talked of God's purpose etcetera but I didn't want to listen. I didn't need him or what he was selling. I had to figure things out on my own.

Danny offered to take me home when he noticed me crying on his shoulder and I accepted. I was tired and wanted to forget this day. We drove through the south side on our way back passing the southside Dairy Queen. I noticed that we were about to pass Brittany's old apartment among the rest of the small project home development that she and her mom had lived in that we used to drop her off at after basketball games. It may have been the pure alcohol that gave a boost of confidence but I suddenly screamed for Danny to stop the car.

My tears started flowing again and I was overcome by a huge weight on my chest. It was hard to breathe even. I opened the door and got out telling Danny to wait at the curb. My hands were trembling but I just had to do this. I had to tell Britt's mom I was sorry. That I didn't mean to abandon her. We didn't know. I didn't know she would disappear from us. I never found the courage to attend Britt's funeral that day. It was just too much and I didn't have it in me then like I do now to go say sorry to Britt's mom. It was a confidence out of tortured guilt that I guess possessed me at this moment. This moment being 6 am now in the morning.

I reached the steps and made my way down the long dark hallway that was dimly lit. I could hear a few dogs barking through the walls with each apartment door I passed. I was a long way from the suburbs. Britt had always talked about the poverty and living conditions she had lived in compared to mine whenever she came and slept over at my house. Now I was seeing up close and personal what she meant. It was a different world. I had immediate gratitude well up in me for where I lived as I finally got to her apartment number and stopped. I took a deep breath and then knocked on the door. I was trembling but I had to confront her. I had to get closure even if it was just with Britt's mom. A minute passed as I kept knocking but no response. I stopped and turned away defeated as I started to make my way down the long-faded hallway. Suddenly, I could hear the bolt lock being twisted and the door opened a jar as I turned back. Britt's mom slowly peeked her head out squinting her eyes at me to focus. I noticed she had dark bags under her eyes and could already smell the fumes of the vodka seconds after opening her door. After her eyes adjusted, her face then had transformed to hate once she got her bearings on who I actually was. Without a beat or time to react, she opened the door all the way and staggered quickly over to me and struck me hard across the face, striking me to the floor.

I held my cheek in pain looking back up at her. She was standing directly over me now. Both of us were now wearing tears.

"How dare you come in here," Britt's mom said with a tone that was just raw.

"How dare you show your face at me," Britt's mom said. I managed to squeak some words out.

"...I...I am sorry. I just wanted to come tell you that....and that I didn't mean to leave her..." Brittany's mom knelt down eye level with me now.

"Brittany should have known better than to trust white folk like you. She should have never gone to that school and met you or she'd be here right now with me I know it! " Britt's mom said. I broke down. Britt's mom upon seeing this did as well but then pure anger consumed her and she lunged at me.

"She would be here with me!" Britt's mom said at the top of her lungs. She then proceeded to pound me as she sat on top of me. She drove her fists all over me as I struggled to get in the fetal position. Moments later, I was saved by Danny. He had come inside with a bad feeling to investigate and ran over pulling Britt's mom off me. I sat up and began to run, wiping the tears away so I could see. Danny followed behind and Britt's mom pursued us. We reached Danny's car and got in just in time to lock the doors. Brittany's mom met me at the passenger window as I buckled my seatbelt and continued to yell profanity at me as she pounded on the glass speeding away.

The ride to my house was silent. I sat there like a zombie as the early morning sun glistened through the car windows. My eyeliner had exploded all over my face. I knew I had asked for what I got by going there. I was hoping for another result. I was hoping for a hug of understanding and for her to forgive me for what I did to her daughter but I guess that wasn't going to be the case. Maybe I thought deep down I knew that and I was going there to punish myself.

Danny pulled into my empty driveway and we sat there in silence. A thunderstorm had moved in fast on our commute home and I sat there watching the rain dance down the windshield in intricate patterns. I wanted to disappear and Danny wanted to pray with me. He took my hand and began praying but I was turned to stone. I couldn't listen to it. In the middle of his prayer for me, I got out and slammed the car door in his face and ran through the rain inside.

Moments later, I burst through my bedroom door clutching the gin bottle from my parents' bar cabinet and plopped on the bed. I hate gin but it went with the theme of the caliche moment. I hated myself at this point and that was all there was to drink. Early in the morning or not, I took a long gulp and began coughing. It burned but if it could numb me, I'd take it. I sat up feeling queasy and made my way to my window. I look out to see my cul-de-sac covered in the downpour. The street ricocheted with raindrops. As I watched the rain fall, I then fell into a total daze and took another pull of my parents' gin bottle. I squirmed, swallowing it down, and wiping my mouth with my free hand. I looked down to see Danny was still parked in my driveway sitting idly by. He hadn't gone home yet. He was still praying for me.

Chapter 17
Brittany Johnson

I came to and opened my eyes. My vision was still blurry but as it went in to focus all I saw was a sea of bright blue. A truck door slammed and I heard footsteps come round the rusted-out truck bed that I now lay in. I immediately reached for the back of my head feeling blood. I winced in pain. It hit me suddenly and I realized I had been struck in the back of the head by that figure from the pursuing truck. There was a thud sound and the back truck bed opened at my feet. The sea of blue that covered me was a blue tarp that was pulled away in a flash leaving me exposed to what I saw – my abductor. It was him, the man watching me from across the street earlier from the theater. Reality set in and I began to scream. Instantly, my mouth met a strip of duct tape that silenced me. My abductor reached in and pulled me out as I was kicking and screaming through my tape. I made a mess of his back tail bed kicking lawn equipment and trash all over the place in protest of him.

I finally saw him face to face for a few minutes as he bound my hands and feet. It clicked, running a jolt of fear down my spine. He was the man I saw years ago that had chased me. I recognized his sheepish face and piercing eyes like it was yesterday. Only now he was older and withered away. Time had not been good to him. His toothy grin revealed stained teeth. His body stunk of booze, dirt, and body odor. He wore an old crusty pair of coveralls as before many years ago. That had not changed. He hoisted me over his shoulder while I started to look around in panic but realized it still must be early morning or late evening and nobody was stirring about. It was pitch black outside except for the little back porch light that lit my abductor's back patio door. A gateway to hell as it would later turn out. We made our way inside his dingy little house. It smelled of mold, old grease, and cigarettes. We reached a door in the middle of his short hallway. He opened it and we started down a dark basement stairwell but of course I didn't go without a fight. I had managed to get my hands free from his tape and grabbed the door frame with both hands holding on for dear life. I began kicking my legs and I could tell he was starting to struggle with me even more so. I had a feeling that if I went down those stairs, I wasn't ever going to go back up them. He finally got so frustrated that he grabbed a hold of me and plum tossed me down the whole flight of stairs like a sack of potatoes. I blacked out.

I opened my eyes barely conscious to see I was being dragged across the dirt floor of the dark lit room. Two wide eyed little girls with gaunt faces covered in dirt and matted hair, stared at me from across the other side of the little basement room in their own separate cages. They looked no older than me. The wire grated door to my cage slam shut in my face. My abductor locked my cage and left us staring at each other in the quiet below with the little ceiling bulb light he had left on shining dimly from the low ceiling. I cried for a long time with my face in my knees. I finally passed out from exhaustion.

I awoke hours later to see my neighbors in their cages still staring at me. Early morning beams of little sunlight began to peek through the crack in the old ground level basement windows that had been blocked out by old and crusted cardboards cutouts.

"How did he get to you?" the one girl asked to my right. She looked about my age either fifteen or sixteen years old. She was Hispanic and through the dirt and grime all over her she looked like she was a pretty girl with natural beauty. The other girl that sat in a welded fastened chicken coup to her left was around the same age but was a blondish little white girl that I had to squint to see that she was indeed blond from all the dirt and grime that covered her.

"Did he get you alone? By yourself?" the girl asked again. I would come to learn that the Hispanic girl was named Ericka Perez. The name hit me instantly. She was taken over two years ago when I was in eighth grade from two counties over. It was a big fuss as she came from a prominent Latino family in the area with strong ties to Mexico. Ericka's disappearance was all over the news for weeks and in our papers with missing signs that even blanketed our town of Gilbertson for months until they all blew away and vanished…kind of like her. I do remember her though. She ran track in junior high and played basketball. She was fast and a natural athlete. Apparently not fast enough for our predator. I always remembered her great smile on the basketball court when we faced her team. That smile was gone now on both of their faces though.

"He took me one night when I was at my Abuelo's house," Ericka muttered. "I was sitting on the front porch with my grandma and watched him mow our church that sat across the street for over an hour. My grandma went inside to get us something to eat and he came over and approached me. Another hour later I was here." Ericka's head sank in defeat when she told me this.

The dirty blond headed girl was named Samantha or Sam. She mentioned to me later on that she had been taken when she was twelve up in Texarkana on the Texas/Arkansas border. She had been left in the car of the grocery store parking lot with the doors unlocked one night while her mother had gone into the store to grab a few quick things. When she came back, she saw her car door wide open and her daughter was gone. Samantha had been missing for four years now.

Both of my new basement friends apologized for how they looked but said it was unavoidable here. Sam and Ericka told me they get let out one by one to go take a shower in his bathroom twice a year. Otherwise, they are here and only taken upstairs to be used once every couple of weeks or so. They told me his sexual encounters with them were becoming less frequent though now over these past years and that his overall health and energy had been subsiding. Obviously abducting Sam in Texarkana meant he was willing to travel and apparently did so at great distances to go do his hunting. Sam and Ericka knew when he would be traveling. That is when they would expect the large buckets of dried food and large buckets for their bathroom use to come out. They were like dogs and I was now to be one of them.

"Are there others? Have there ever been others beside you two…or me down here?" I asked on our second evening still getting a grasp of my new world. They told me that there had been dozens of others down here but they didn't last long. They would either fade away due to the health conditions and or would just never be quiet and he would finally have enough of it. He would come down and snatched them out of their cages dragging them upstairs never to be seen again. I had a strong belief nobody ever saw them again for that matter. "You have to stay quiet and don't look at him.

That's how we survive down here," Sam said.

"That and you have to keep some kind of hope…or you will kill yourself down here. Not him."

They told me also that they never get used to when he takes advantage of them but it does get easier to block it out when it does happen. I began to cry hearing this as I lay in my corner eating the dried food from a bowl that had been laid out for me.

"It's weird, 'cause like…it's almost like when he uses us it's his fuel. It's his source of food alone," Ericka uttered. "When he takes us upstairs and uses us it's usually then when he has the strength to go and be gone for days. There's an evil in him that is deeper than you have ever known. It's an evil that is not human. That is what is the scariest part when I am with him," Ericka admitted. We ate the rest of our meal from our bowls in silence that third evening. All the talking must have worn them out as they slept most of the time for days after that.

The days and nights slowly started to blur together and a deep sadness and depression sank into me. Something deeper and more sour than I had ever known or experienced dealing with Momma and her misery. If anything, I missed her grief momma brought me. I wanted that back and would take it in a heartbeat. I had all the time in the world now to replay everything and every minute of my life as I sat in that cage. I would often go back to that night I was taken, wondering what I could have done differently. If I had only chosen to do something else that night, would I still have ended up here? If I've gone to see my grandparents instead of going with Kristen that night, would I still have ended up here eventually? What if I was never friends with Kristen Brooks? The fear now always flooded my mind with the thoughts of dread to think if I ever would leave this place. Will I ever step outside of this house ever again? Time would tell.

That's all I had now. Time.

Chapter 18
Kristen Brooks

I sat in my old Honda Civic and stared at the neon naked woman sign glowing at me through my rainy driver's side window. It was now a little over three years since Brittany had been abducted. I was finishing my freshman year at UT in Austin and had a few weeks left before the summer. Everything went as planned. I left Gilbertson last August, packed my little Honda, and drove to the big city and exhaled a huge breath pulling out of the city limits. Danny and I broke up last summer as well. I can't say that I didn't see it coming. We all did. He had found Jesus and I had found anything that could distract me at eye level. I definitely wasn't looking upward. He kissed me goodbye in my driveway and I got in my car to drive to Austin and he got in his car to drive to the airport. He was going to start some missionary training program. "I'll be praying for you!" He shouted as I was pulling away. I left him and Ross watching me go as I pulled out of our cul-de-sac. I cried the whole way to my dorm.

I was lost then and feel even more so now. I was looking for the fulfillment of that void. That gap that was created by the lack of family and guilt of Brittany's disappearance. After the holidays this past year, I moved in with my dorm roommate, Tera, into a two-bedroom apartment on the south side of Austin. Tera was a wild one who was very smart, attractive, and definitely living for the experience of college and not so much the education part of it. She was also very persuasive to an extent. She had talked me out of quitting my job at the outlet mall a few months ago and getting a job with her at a gentlemen's club as a cocktail waitress for the monetary value. Hence, why I am here now sitting out in my car in the rain staring at a neon naked woman on a sign and dreading it. I have been working here for a month or so now. I have to say I was not really fond of the gawking looks over my body that I get every night, but the money was absolutely great for a college kid on her own and the culture here always left you wasted by the end of the night with all the drinks you could want to help you forget about the baggage in Gilbertson. To say I was now an alcoholic was an understatement. I knew it but didn't care. The alcohol numbed me and that is what I wanted....It was safe to say that I was a long way from nursing that gin bottle while watching Danny in the driveway that one evening over a year ago.

I let out a sigh and knew it was time. I had to go in and start my shift. I glossed my lips one more time and did a hair check in the overhead mirror, of course why bother as it was raining, and stepped out into the downpour in my heels towards the front door of "The Neon Lady Gentlemen's Club."

It was always the same. The club music hit me in the face the moment I stepped in. I could smell the stale cigarette smoke mixed with the dancers' exotic perfume. I said hello to my bouncer crew as I walked past the front check in and went to put my purse up behind the bar. Tera was already there and in true Tera fashion while mid act of slamming a shot with one of the bartenders. She laughed and let out a yell giving me a high five as I approached. As usual, I fell right in line and took my first tequila shot for the night. You have to get in the right mindset for the rush that was coming. An hour from now this place would be packed. Twenty-five girls or more would be taking turns hitting the stage for their routine pole dances and getting groped and molested by men doing lap dances for them in the dark corners of the club. The club had many dark corners. Not to mention my own backside would be slapped many times in passing as though that was a normal thing to do. It was not very gentlemanly for a gentleman's club but as long as it paid, I didn't care.

The evening flew by and it was already 3 am without me realizing it. When you are taking shots of tequila and being pressured to do bumps of coke, it tends to happen. The work crew consisted of the manager, bouncers, bartenders and waitstaff all gathered around the bar having our own party and letting off steam from the night of work. The laughter and yelling escalated to a decimal point that my ears would permanently ring for the next three days. I found it funny that when it was just us staff at the end of the night, we still blared the music to the highest volume inside the club.

An hour later, a group of ten of us from the club were all standing in the middle of Tera and I's kitchen back at our apartment continuing to laugh and scream. I was having trouble standing to be honest. I was beyond drunk but Tera kept supplying the peer pressure at me to keep going. Pills of Molly were passed out around the staff right before we left to come back to our apartment so now everyone was in that vibe. Hands were wandering everywhere on everyone and a guy with a red beard whom I had never met before kept close to me and touched me everywhere. Constantly. Standing there in the kitchen island, I felt my pulse raise and my body go numb. I was hot and starting to faint. I remember the red beard leaned over whispering something in my ear and then…black.

I awoke to a direct sunbeam piercing through one of my bedroom window shades hitting me directly head on as I lay passed out on my stomach and working on a nice collection of drool beside my head. I could hear the highway outside as well as snoring that wasn't my own. I was naked and still covered in sweat. My head pounded and I was fearing the worst. I leaned over to look behind me to see the red beard himself snoring away and completely exposed. I wanted to vomit and needed to anyway. What had happened? There was no memory of how I got here much less how the red bearded dragon did either.

I sat up, holding the vomit in my mouth, and trotted into the bathroom shutting the door behind me to relieve myself. I was hurting all over and was gutted. I was mad at myself for being in this position. For getting to that state last night. I knew I was starting to lose control a bit. I had not slept with anyone since pre-Christian Danny and wasn't planning to. Now who knows who all I slept with last night. I couldn't tell you. I started a hot shower and stood there in a trance as the water hit my face. Twenty minutes went by and I must have fallen asleep while standing there. The water became cold and shook me awake. I then dried off with a towel and swallowed a mouthful of Tylenol and put the lid down on my toilet to take a seat. I could still hear red beard cutting logs through the door. I looked over to see my phone on the bathroom counter and grabbed it. It was 2:30 in the afternoon. I saw a voicemail from this morning. It was from mom.

Oh joyous.

Mom and dad, as per usual, had yet to make it up to see me at college my freshman year. They were too busy to drive me to freshman orientation so I wasn't surprised. The voicemail was of mom scolding me over this semester's grades or lack thereof, and that her and dad would cut my tuition off if I didn't pull them up. It was surprising to see mom take such a strong interest in my grades anyway. Screw my parents is all I thought to myself. While debating on what to do about red beard, I sat on my toilet seat and got sucked down the rabbit hole of social media on my phone. Before too long, I was on Brittany's Facebook page scrolling through our old high school photos of her and I. It couldn't be helped. The tears started to flow and feeling bad already with a hangover from hell didn't help either. I wondered where she was right now. Was she trapped in a bathroom like I was? Was she at college somewhere? Was she alive?

Chapter 19
Brittany Johnson

It was early still when I rolled off of my dirt covered mattress on to my knees.

I made it an everyday habit to pray when I woke. It had been nearly over a year now that I had been abducted and came to be a prisoner here. I prayed the same little prayer I always prayed every morning. I prayed for patience, confidence, strength, and most overall – peace. I prayed that God would give me peace so that it would stay here within me while I was down here in this place. Looking back later, down there in that cage in those times was the closest I had ever been to God. I had to go to a dungeon to find him and truly see and feel his presence. After all, I really did have all the time in the world to be still and know that he is the Lord. It's funny how outside of this cage you get caught up in all the busyness of the world that you never then stop to truly be with God. I'm here and HE is all I have and all I cling to for hope. Otherwise, I knew I would die.

I said amen to myself and sat up reaching for my bowl of food left over for me.

The other girls were up but not speaking or acknowledging each other. Most of the time we were too weak to communicate. We mostly stayed to ourselves unless he, the abductor, got us fired up over something he had done earlier. Sam had developed a severe cough that I was afraid was turning into or was now full-blown pneumonia. I could tell it was weighing on the abductor upstairs on what to do with her. I feared in the back of my mind she would die. I prayed for her constantly but knew her fate may not be a good one unless something was done.

During the day we were given our rations to eat and books to read here and there. I of course had my bible I had discovered in the dirt which became my sword. It guarded my heart and mind in this place and I chose to absorb myself in it. To immerse myself in it as it was all I had. I felt it was a lamp given to me for this underground darkness. His word had been saving me daily. Each morning I read a few psalms to Ericka in her cage next to me. She had started coming around and asking for a psalm read to her every day. She said it was comforting and helped with a routine which was what you had to do to fill the days and not get overwhelmed with being lost and losing all hope.

My routine was simple but followed with discipline. Every morning I woke and prayed and read psalms. Then I ate whatever dried food was left in my bowl. Usually then it was bathroom time. We all had gotten used to going in front of one another. The girls were not fazed as I was the new one on the block. However, after three days of awkwardness in doing my business it then never even crossed my mind again. After the restroom, usually Ericka would stir and we would talk or chat as she ate some of her food. If Sam at this point was well enough, she would join in but lately I fear the pneumonia had set in and she wasn't doing much of anything. She may have moved once or twice a day to go to the bathroom. However, even doing that sent her into a coughing fit that would wipe her out. The rest of the day would be spent either reading or Ericka and I reading to one another. Me reading the Bible and her reading whatever dime store trash romance novel was tossed in her cage. It was quite a contest to read something so X-rated and then read Bible scriptures. It was entertaining at times to say the least.

Some days, usually once a week, he would come down stairs and take one of us up to abuse. Whenever one of us was taken it usually was for an hour or so. Of us left in the basement, it was quiet and you could feel the tension and dread of knowing what was going on above. Sometimes you could hear it if it was bad enough. Then when he was done, we would be flung back in our cage and left to silence. No one would ever say anything. There really was nothing to say. It was quiet except for whoever had just gone up. They were heard crying and sniffling in the dark. Me included if it had been my turn. Ericka was taken the most out of all of us. She was no doubt his favorite. I couldn't tell you the last time he took Sam upstairs. It had been months. She had gotten sick and he wanted no part of it.

On this one particular morning, I was up reading and praying in my cage. The early morning sunbeams shot through the cracks in the covered windows like laser beams cutting the darkness. Suddenly, the basement door at the top of the stairs flew open. He was breathing heavily and speaking in gibberish to himself once again. I could tell he was liquored up and had been out all night. He made a few steps down the stairwell before his legs gave out and he rolled down the rest of the way spilling onto the basement cemented dirt floor in front of us. There were a few seconds of silence. Was he dead? Could we be so lucky? Or was that luck? If he was dead, how would we ever get out of here?

Suddenly he grunted loudly and slowly staggered to his feet. A strong dribble of blood oozed out from his forehead from the fall. He then shuffled over to my cage and fell forward against it falling flat on his face in front of me. He then lifted his head to look at me and from his angle saw my Bible open that was half tucked under my mattress.

He let out a shriek and then got to his knees out of breath. He began to gargle blood as it had drained down to his mouth from his forehead. With half shut eyes, he stared at me and grinned a bloody grin.

"Why little bird…what you got there in that cage?"

He made a gesture to my Bible below me. "You think he gonna save you?

Uh? Your God gonna save you down here?" he teased.

He then leaned towards my cage placing his dirt and grime fingers through the chicken wire.

"Your mine. Nobody's comin' for you little bird. You're my property now. If that God of yours is so powerful, then tell him to show. Come on tell 'em!" he yelled at me.

He then spat blood on my face but I dare not look away. I stared a hole right back into his empty eyes.

"He is here…and that's the one thing you can't take from me," I said. "I'm gonna pray for you. By the look of ya, you need all the prayer you can get," I said sternly.

When I said this, he suddenly went wild like a wild animal having convulsions. It was like something not of this earth had gripped him. He fumbled with the lock but then grabbed me violently with one arm flinging me out of my cage sending me flying into Ericka and Sam's. We all started to scream now. He began to scream as well, mocking us. He then with one arm back handed me across the face knocking me back to the ground. He tossed me over his shoulder and we started the slow ascent up the stairs for him to have his way. Earlier that morning, I had read and memorized Psalm 62. As he carried me up those basement steps, the psalm organically came to my lips.

1...Truly my soul finds rest in God; my salvation comes from him. 2 Truly he is my rock and my salvation; he is my fortress, I will never be shaken. 3 How long will you assault me? Would all of you throw me down – this leaning wall, this tottering fence? 4 Surely, they intend to topple me from my lofty place; they take delight in lies. With their mouths they bless, but in their hearts they curse. 5 Yes, my soul, find rest in God; my hope comes from him. 6 Truly he is my rock and my salvation; he is my fortress, I will not be shaken. 7 My salvation and my honor depend on God; he is my mighty rock, my refuge. Trust in him at all times, you people; pour out your hearts to him, for God is our refuge. 8 Trust in him at all times, you people; pour out your hearts to him, for God is our refuge. 9 Surely the lowborn are but a breath, the highborn are but a lie. If weighed on a balance, they are nothing; together they are only a breath. 10 Do not trust in extortion or put vain hope in stolen goods; though your riches increase, do not set your heart on them. 11 One thing God has spoken, two things I have heard: "Power belongs to you, God, 12 and with you, Lord, is unfailing love," and, "You reward everyone according to what they have done."

Chapter 20
Kristen Brooks

I sat isolated in the back corner of the room that was covered with mirrors. It was a dressing room that stunk of exotic perfume and musty beer and cigarettes. I sunk into my chair thinking of the night that lay ahead for me. I yawned as I worked on my eye liner. It had been a year now since I had come to work as a waitress at The Neon Naked Lady. I was on autopilot now. I was in cruise control heading downward about to crash into the big mountain. I hadn't spoken to my parents in six months and school was definitely nonexistent now. I had dropped out after my freshman year. I had been permanently drunk and strung out on drugs basically for the past month. For the past two weeks now, I decided to crank it up a notch and knew I needed to support my lifestyle and drug habit so I went upon the motivation of my work peers and was dancing now at the Neon Naked Lady. I had a pole routine and everything. Bruises covered my whole body from the touching and harassment of the 'gentlemen' patrons night after night. I was lost but not really caring about being found.

Suddenly, I heard my name from the voice that made me wince every time he said it. It was DJ Vic on the mic announcing it was my turn to take the main center stage. I hurriedly strapped on my clear acrylic five-inch heels that was the fashion and slammed the two white lines that were on the counter in front of me like a railroad track. My nose burned as I staggered over to the stairs to take the stage. Vic cued up my music and in a few minutes' time, I laid naked on the stage floor in front of a dozen drunken men being showered by dollar bills. I was high. I was drunk and visibly numb inside and out, and I was a long way from my cul-de-sac in Gilbertson.

Minutes later, my songs ended and I exited the stage. Gathering my clothes where I could find them, I made my way to the back bar to slam a tequila shot. I wanted to make sure I stayed numb. A portly guy with long hair and a familiar bearded face approached me asking for a VIP exclusive in one of the back rooms. I didn't object. It was usually me, the stripper, having to bounce around all night on different guys' laps begging to give me attention and a dance. Meanwhile they would be getting free feels all over me while I negotiated the lap dance.

I told the bearded guy sure and we made our way to the VIP room to do things that went way over extended just a lap dance unfortunately. I didn't care though. I drank enough each night to make sure I could barely remember…or care. We made our way into the private room where he immediately became aggressive. My clothes were off in seconds and he had me gripped tight in his grasp on his lap. He pulled my hair suddenly a little too hard and I let out a scream and cursed him as I flew off his lap. It was there in that brief sobering moment that I realized who this familiar face was.

"Kristen, I am sorry," he pleaded. "I am sorry if I hurt you. I…"

"Mr. Shilling?!" I gasped.

Mr. Shilling was my 8th grade science teacher that all the girls had a crush on and let us retake our midterms when we flunked them. Now he was this overweight bearded guy who had just touched all over my naked body and seemed prone to abuse.

"Yeah. Look, I love you, Kristen. I always have. Even back then. When I heard you were dancing up here in Austin, I had to…"

"Oh my God," I said. Not giving him another second, I left him with his pants half unbuckled and walked out totally disgusted. I pushed the back exit door open to the staff only outside smoking patio and lit up a cigarette. I took a drag and exhaled out slowly trying to shake off the encounter I just had. What a creep.

Suddenly, I heard familiar laughter coming from the other end of the parking lot. I turned to see my roommate, Tera, making her way arm and arm in some cocktail dress and ducking into a Lamborghini that had been parked out front. Seconds later the engine flared up and revved and then the car was gone. For the past few months now, I had seen Tera less and less at home and or at the club. She had found a site online for high end escorts and after doing her research she thought it was more lucrative financially. She had been selling me on it the past few weeks to forget going into dancing and look into this as the money seemed amazing. Before I could put out my cigarette, the door burst open and it was Mr. Shilling himself who had been hunting for me all throughout the club. Before he could say anything, I ran past him back inside and left while letting management know I was done for the evening due to a stalker.

Needless to say, Mr. Shilling was banned from the establishment now.

It was later that night I found myself at my kitchen counter in my apartment scrolling on my old laptop. The escort service site was up and I was perusing. It had been just a couple weeks and dancing naked for money was getting old. Very old. Plus, I couldn't make enough, it seemed to support my habits that I needed. Then with perfect timing, the front door buzzed and then opened. Tera came prancing holding shopping bags and a fresh bottle of high-end liquor. She came into the kitchen plopping down on the counter next to me.

"Awwww, someone's back on the 'Love Me' site again," Tera said. Noticing my laptop. She ripped open the bottle cap of booze and took a huge chug and then handed it to me.

"See this is where it's at. You get to set your own hours. You have a select pool of clientele, aaaand they buy you cool stuff from time to time," Tera bragged, lifting up her Nieman Marcus bag.

"Yeah, but do you actually have sex with these guys?" I asked. I already knew the answer.

"Kris. What do you think? It ain't all that bad," Tera said, lifting the bottle again. I stared at the site and tried to visualize. Could it be that bad?

I opened my eyes and sat up gasping. Where was I? It was dark, I was groggy, and I couldn't recognize the geography of the dark room around me. This was becoming a common way to wake unfortunately. It had been three months since that night in the kitchen with Tera. I was a full-on escort now. I had a few steady clients but there were a lot of random hook ups that led to random places I found myself in. Hotel rooms to lofts to married guys' houses in the suburbs and waking up to see pictures of my client's wife and kids all staring back at me.

At this particular moment, I woke up in a high-rise hotel room on the west side of Austin. It was fairly nice with a gorgeous view of the lake poking through the blinds.

What wasn't so gorgeous was the view I witnessed on the other side of me sharing the bed. Next to me laid a very large, hairy, and balding man snoring away. He smelled and instantly, drunken images of him on me came to the surface. I immediately rose out of bed bare naked and sprinted to the bathroom to vomit as I usually did. I came out of the bathroom and poured myself some leftover champagne out of the bucket on the table to help settle my body shakes. I walked to the window and peaked out on the gorgeous view of the lake that spread over the beautiful Texas Hill Country below me. The guerilla was still in the bed fast asleep. I stood there for a while daydreaming out the window. I thought about home and what mom and dad were up to. I thought about my brother Ross and if he would be going to college soon or not. We too had not spoken in the past year. I never took his calls. I missed them terribly but wouldn't let myself admit that. I chugged the rest of my champagne and grabbed my clothes. I wanted to get out of here. I wanted to be alone. I wanted to be off drugs. I wanted to stop drinking. I wanted to go back to school. I wanted to see my family. I wanted a lot of things. Right now…I wanted to sleep.

Chapter 21
Abaddon

My captive consumed glass after glass of water quenching his thirst. We had been up together way before dawn dealing with our little problem. It was yesterday that we found ourselves four counties over from the town side of Gilbertson on one of our regular hunts. We had an opportunity late yesterday afternoon at dusk and stumbled upon a young girl that was found in the solitary confines of her backyard. We were able to capture and overcome our new found victim but were surprised by fight and vigor. My captive physically had to restrain her many times but with no true success. She was finally strangled to death by my captive in an alleyway in the bed of his truck. Now all we had was a body and body that indeed needed to be discarded immediately. Over the past four years ever since our victim numbers continued to increase, the authorities of the surrounding counties increased their pursuits as well.

It was then an hour later, we had discarded the young female body to the bottom of the Brazos River. Callan, my captive, had tied a rope to a large rock from the river bed and then attached it to our failed young female's ankle. She was then tossed over the bridge and my captive and myself I must admit, caught our breath in relief. There had been many failures over the years such as this but this was a tough one, I must admit. It was that but also the fact that my captive was indeed weakening from my long presence. I knew our end together would be coming to an end one day. Soon perhaps.

We had made it back now to my captive's dwelling as the sun rose finding ourselves where we are currently at the kitchen sink. My captive set his empty glass in the sink and wiped his mouth wiping sweat away from his brow and looked out the kitchen window. He knew his body needed rest. However, I had other plans for him. We needed to keep hunting. Yesterday was a failure and I needed another fuel source. We badly needed a new captive prisoner for the basement below. It had been years now since we dragged the body of the fallen one from the basement below. One of Callan's first prisoner's, Samantha Howitzer, had finally expired. Disease and inflammation of the lungs had finally taken hold and she had begun to stink in my captive's basement and therefore was removed. That was eight years ago. Therefore, we were in bad need for new reinforcements to join the rest in the basement below. Callan, my captive, could sleep later today. We needed to go out on patrol to look for the next one right now.

My captive went below to the basement, fed his current prisoners while also changing out their chamber pots, and then refueled his lawn equipment. We could work and hunt at the same time. That was common protocol. Callan and I then slipped into his truck and slowly pulled away from his little house that kept all of my dark little secrets.

It was a particularly hot morning for a mid-June day in the southern region of Texas. My captive had soaked through his coveralls with last night's misfortunes so he now wore jeans and a stained t-shirt as a substitute. He ripped from a fresh cigarette as we cruised down the backroads of Gilbertson heading towards a job but taking the long way in case we happen upon a fortunate prey that is alone and vulnerable. Those opportunities were becoming less and less these days again causing us to travel farther distances.

As we made our way to the west end, we approached such luck. It was when we turned on Travis Street passing the small Gilbertson Bible church. It was a small quaint church that we had yet to infiltrate. There were over thirty churches in the small city and we had our talons in maybe half. This Bible church here was a new prospect. My captive turned in and parked along the curb by the church's side yard that faced the street. It was there we saw our vision. There, sitting on a park bench by the side door sat a young girl in her teens occupied on her cellar device as though she was waiting for someone. Alone. What luck.

I do say that I love the new advances of this technological world we are creating.

My Lordship is its number one sponsor and supporter I can tell you. Cellphones, laptops, social media. It was all such a great weapon to help grasp and isolate the souls we wanted to take. All of this technology is vastly propelling forward such isolation, anxiety, and distraction from The Creator as well as humans themselves. My kind for his Lordship was reaping all the benefits from it. Case in point, the girl before us sat stuck on her cellular totally distracted from her surroundings. It is a perfect opportunity to strike.

My captive, Mr. Callan Sullivan, stepped out of his truck quietly putting out his cigarette on the street and grooming himself in his rear-view mirror. He then stepped to the curb and made his way to the sidewalk to begin our pursuit of our prey on the church bench. Moments later we were by her side. She had yet to look up from her phone and as we approached, she was startled. My captive's appearance wasn't in his best form so I myself now had to turn on the inner charm.

"Pardon me ma'am. I'm sorry I didn't mean to startle ya. I saw ya sittin' over here," Cal uttered to her while looking sheepishly at the ground. The girl stood up and countered one step back away from Cal.

"No, it's okay. You just startled me," the young girl said off balance.

Cal let out an eerie raspy smoker's laugh. "Yeah, I know it! I done sneaked up on ya! You were glued to that phone there." Cal stated, still laughing. A moment of silence went by that translated to awkwardness. Cal just stared at her fixated.

"Can I help you sir?" the girl asked.

"Uh yeah, I was wonderin' who I'd ask on who cuts this here lawn? That's what I do. See that's my truck. Got my stuff in there. See." Cal said pointing to the curb where his truck was parked.

"I can help you!" a voice cried from the church building. Cal turned to see a young thirty something dirty blonde headed lady with kind eyes approaching them. I could tell she entered our conversation with caution and was on alert given our presence. Damn. We missed our opportunity here with this young victim. With any luck, we would have gotten her by my captive's truck where we may have been able to subdue her if the opportunity presented itself. Now that was off the table.

The young woman was named Pastor Kristen Brooks. She is the new hire pastor here for this church and from what I can tell was originally a local from the area. She deflected from our pursuit of the younger girl and excused her to answer what questions we may have had. I kept focus so as to have my captive stay professional and appear genuine in speech during this transaction of communication. Pastor Brooks addressed our inquiries and suggested that she would be willing to hire us on for a trial period.

Their lawn man had just moved and the timing was perfect. It was perfect indeed. We had now yet another congregation that we could get close to infiltrate at any weak link we could find in said congregation. This in the long run today may have turned out more fortunate for our efforts than planned. We still need to fill our basement but…all good things come to those that wait..

Chapter 22
Brittany Johnson

I laid in my cage with my head to the dirt floor. I had become weak. I had been losing hope. I stared at the dirty Bible that lay in the corner of my cage. It has been months now since I opened it. I was struggling. It had been eight years since Sam had finally died of pneumonia. I still remember the image of him dragging her lifeless body up the stairs never to be seen again. Some girls over the coming years then came and filled Sam's cage but went due to making so much noise and fighting him too much. He would give up and just take them away back up those stairs and we would never see them again.

Ericka was staying strong but had lost a lot of weight. Most likely stomach worms because her diet hadn't changed much. She still looked tired and skinny to the bone. As the years went by, I found ourselves talking to each other less and less. I think part of that was the hope being let out of us too much less just sheer energy to do so. A week ago, he came down the stairs in a rant and a mood and had chosen me. We went upstairs for one of our usual sessions but he was very physical this time. It was then over two hours later that he poured me back into my cage. I could barely breathe. My body was limp and hurt all over. I couldn't move. That is when the true darkness had started to take hold of me down here. I stopped eating, I stopped reading, and I stopped even praying. I became too weak to do anything. I had given up on everything. The hope was gone. I had made it nine years and then some down here but had reached my max.

As the darkness crawled further over me, I began to hallucinate. I would call to Pappy and Momma thinking they were right outside my cage letting me out. I would see visions of them from time to time that I swore was real. I would then break out into hysterical shrieking as my eyesight started to go out. Ericka would muster as much energy as she could to calm me down from where she lay but she could only do so much for so long. On the seventh day of not eating or drinking and just lying in my own mess, I started to pass on. I remember drawing a few last heavy breaths in as though I was crawling and scrambling to keep my grasp from falling off a long dark cliff. I then let go.

It was then that I reached into a heavier darkness. However, I felt more alert now. I could breathe easier now and the air was pure. It was cool and calm now in this new darkness. Suddenly, a light showed above me that was almost blinding and it absorbed me, swallowing me up. I was then standing in an open grass field. I was full of energy now and felt no more pain from my body that now appeared to be clean. Looking around I could see two eight-foot-tall creatures of golden and bronze skin that were not of this world. They had white wings and were walking alongside me twenty yards apart from me or so as I paced through the tall green grass. The scenery was amazing. There were mountains and flowers of different beautiful colors all around me. Some colors I had never seen before.

In the distance on the sides of these hills and mountains, I could make out village dwellings of beautiful size.

After walking for several minutes in amazement by all the vibrant beauty that surrounded me, I saw him. I knew instantly who he was. I just knew. He stood wearing an all-white robe fifty yards straight ahead of me with open arms. Without thinking I ran to him. I was immediately attracted to him and longed to touch and hug him. We embraced and I looked up at him as we embraced. He was a natural man and more rugged looking than how we depict him. However, there is a kindness in his eyes that is captivating. I didn't want to look away from them once I locked eyes upon his. He smiled at me and I knew I was home. I was in the presence of Jesus.

We separated from each other and we stood there silent gazing at one another. Tears began to stream down my face. We spoke to each other without physically saying a word. We didn't have to. We knew each other's thoughts. My first reaction and thought to being in His presence was: "…this is love." That was all I was thinking when we first approached each other. I immediately felt all the love and fulfillment that I didn't while on earth. I knew then after seeing him where I was now too.

He took my hand and we began to walk along a river or flowing creek that appeared. I don't know how to describe it. It sounds crazy but the river itself was almost flowing through him. It was the river of life. It was an image that is hard to describe in how we see things on earth. Seeing this told me as well that this was indeed heaven and a much different place. Yet from the qualities of the river and mountains that surrounded me, I could tell this place and earth all had the same maker. As we walked, he asked how I was and he knew I had had a hard past couple of years.

"You know that I have been with you during that time?" He asked me. I nodded and said of course I knew. I was glad he was there. As we walked and held hands, I asked him about my dad. Was he here? It was then that he looked up and pointed passed my shoulder smiling. I turned slowly not expecting what I would see. It was here across the meadow on the other side of the river I could make out both my daddy and momma. They were holding hands and waving at me. They both seemed younger and more vibrant too. I could make out that they were actively busy with a group of people sitting around a banquet table. I could hear their laughter from across the field. My eyes welled up again and I cried. I cried tears of pure joy. My parents were happy. They were together. That meant Momma had passed while I was down there in that basement if she was now here with daddy. It probably was finally the drink that killed her mixed with the depression of losing me and daddy, but now she was happy. She looked younger, healthier, and calm now.

I turned back to see Jesus again. "Your parents are both here now," he said. "I have prepared a place for them just as I have prepared a place for you but it is not your time to dwell here in this place quite yet," Jesus said.

I asked him why. Where was I to go? I am here now. He told me my time was not finished. He said I was to go and keep proclaiming his name and that I had his work that was yet to be finished. I pleaded with Jesus as I didn't want to go back. I didn't want to go back to that dark place. He again assured me he would be with me and that I would not always be in that dark basement.

"You will one day be free my love. And when you are, go and claim my name in all things," Jesus said to me.

And with that he hugged me and before I knew it, I looked down at my feet to see I was now sitting in a canoe like raft floating down the river of life away from him. He waved me goodbye as I began to cry once again. I looked to my right on the other side of the river bank and from a distance saw my parents waving to me as well before turning back to their group. Then in a flash, I was covered in darkness again. I suddenly let out a gasp of air and a mixture of gravity and weight hit me again as I started into a coughing fit. It was dark but I could smell the old and musty smell of the basement now and I knew I was back.

I sat up in my cage and looked at Ericka who looked back at me with wide eyes and total shock.

"I...I thought you were dead. You haven't responded at all in two days Britt," Ericka said.

I was depressed after where I had just come from and seen but I was comforted all at the same time. Biggest thing...I was hungry. I reached over and grabbed my food bowl and water bottle. I began to eat again.

Chapter 23
Kristen Brooks

I tossed and turned in the back of my old Honda for an hour but couldn't sleep. Not tonight. I was itching and needed more but would have to wait four or five hours. It had been over a year and a half since I sat at that kitchen counter letting Tera, my roommate at the time, talk me into going down the rabbit hole of the escort service. Tera and the face value of the escort website was right about the lifestyle and that it could be glamorous. What they forgot to tell me was the baggage and attachments it brought along with it.

I had not seen Tera in over six months nor did I know where she was. We had gotten in a fight while we were both high and it had gotten physical. I couldn't pay the rent to her anymore due to my excessive drug habits now and that had become my main focus. I had been living in my car now for six months since our fight. I ran out of couches to crash on. A few weeks ago, I had pulled by our old place to beg for some money from her and a place to stay for the night that wasn't a stiff car seat but she had gone. There was no sign of her and a family was living in our apartment now.

Any money I made doing 'my work' went to drugs, a little gas, and food when or if I was hungry. I was now fully addicted to crack and alcohol but I would never admit that. The crack escort living in her car in a Target parking lot wouldn't ever admit a rock bottom was now in full effect. Funny, this life description wasn't listed on the escort website either. I had chosen drugs above all else and it now was my only identity. It was 9:30 pm and I was trying to get some sleep before I would get up to find a client to persuade to have sex with me and or hunt for something to smoke. Naturally with my drug habit, my clientele had gone downhill. When grooming is not a priority naturally that can have an effect on your work. I also found myself lately drawn to only clients that had drugs anyway.

Luckily, Omar, who was the Target parking lot security guard, was cool with me. I think he was smart enough to see I was a nice girl but just in a bit of a slump so to speak. He allowed me to park my car on the side of the Target parking lot. It was the holiday season and I would lay there in my passenger seat most nights high and eating a Target food court meal, watching the families hustle in and out of the glowing red building doing their last-minute Christmas shopping before going home to their cozy houses. I would look at each one and wonder where they were going after their shopping. I would make up stories about them and daydream that I could be part of that family if I just went over there and asked for their help and a place to stay. My mind would run away even farther with me and I would then think of home. I wondered how Ross was. Where did he go to college? Did he go? How was mom and dad? Did they really miss me? Or had they forgotten all about me and were now wrapped up and busy with work more than they ever had been. Would my family be celebrating Christmas this year? Were they all together at the house to celebrate or was it just Ross alone while mom and dad were out doing only God knows what for sake of their careers? I would find myself in tears with all these thoughts which caused me to crawl to my back seat and cry myself to sleep in my little car.

My cell phone rang early the next morning. I sat up suddenly in my back seat and winced in pain. I had another crick in my neck from my luxury Honda Civic backseat paradise. The morning sun blinded me as it poured through my back ice frosted passenger side window.

"Hello?" I muttered to my cell.

It was Quentin. He had become my steady drug dealer as well as recruiter for clients. He was a guy I had met on the streets who was your small-time drug dealer but basically homeless himself. I thought he had my best interests at heart and we were friends. We all know that would not end up to be true. Most clients he would bring me were just truckers at the interstate motel that wanted some fun and some drugs and to party. Quentin and I would split the money and he would then supply me my next hit. It was the perfect partnership. Many things about Quentin caused me to have reservations. But the crack said otherwise and that he was perfectly trustworthy. He was so trustworthy in fact that he knew I had been keeping a roll on me, saving up. A roll of money that is. I had for the past couple months grown tired of the car life and wanted to save now and put money down on rent and fix my car.

115

However, it was hard and my habit was taxing. I only had four hundred dollars but my goal was to put it away when I could.

Quentin, always skipped the formal hellos and asked if I could meet at a house address in an hour. He has somebody for me but didn't want to meet at the motel this time. Something seemed anxious and amiss in his voice. I thought it strange too that he didn't want to meet at our usual spot but I went with it. I wanted to eat today and it had been a while since my last hit so I was beginning to feel bad and anxious, myself. I agreed and fired up my Honda after its second false start to go to the address.

It was depressing pulling up to my arrival. It had started to rain of all things and the house looked like a crack den. How appropriate. It most likely was indeed an abandoned house where the homeless lived. It could be Quentin's actual place for all I knew or one of them. I pulled to the curb and let out a sigh as I turned off my car. Was I really going to go in there? A crack house? I was a crackhead now so wasn't it only fitting to do so. I belonged there now in that old dreary abandoned house that sat in front of me. I have come a long way to now belonging to this place. My heart sank with these thoughts running through my mind but then my body took over. I was needing a hit.

I opened my car door and sprinted through the rain to the front porch. I knocked hard hoping Quentin inside would hear my banging through the pounding rain. Moments later I heard the door unlatch and Quentin peaked his head through. He wore a hoodie and I strained to confirm it was actually him. He let out a faint smile and opened the door welcoming me in. I stepped in and took a second to dry my hair and wipe the rain off of my already soaked body. Looking around the place, it was cold, dark and bare. All I could see was scattered trash from squatters that had come and gone from this place. From all I could tell, it was just Quentin and I. He lit an old candle on the mantle with his pocket lighter and turned to face me.

"You find the place okay?" he asked.

"Yeah, no problem. Quentin what is going on? What is this place? Why are we not just meeting at the motel like usual? This isn't cool," I complained.

Quentin made a stride over to me and gave me a cigarette. "Hey be cool baby. This guy wanted to meet in a very secluded spot so this is what it had to be," he said.

"Yeah, I'll say. This place is kind of creeping me out. Very romantic," I said sarcastically, setting my purse down.

"Look, this is my buddy's place so it's fine. Hey, he'll be here shortly so just chill," he said smiling a toothy gold tooth grin. "You and I could have a hit while we wait perhaps?" I asked.

"Oh, you know I am down for that. You got your roll by the way?" he asked nonchalant as he cooked up a hit for us to smoke by candlelight.

"Well….yeah, I always have it on me. I ain't gonna leave it in my car that's for sure," I said.

Quentin lit his crack pipe and took a big drag. "What's that roll up to now anyway?" he asked.

"I don't know…almost five hundred after this weekend. I wanna save a little more and put a down payment on my place," I informed him. Quentin nodded, agreeing. "Alright, that's what's up. I like it. That's dope."

"Why? Why do you ask?" I questioned back.

"Oh nothing. I just wanted to make sure it's worth it," he said.

Upon him saying that I detected movement just behind me. There had been someone else in here with us. I suddenly felt a hard blow to the back of the head that sent me face diving forward to the ground almost blacking out. I then felt stomping and kicking to my face, stomach, and legs. I had been set up and was ambushed. Quentin leaned over me, ripping my money roll from my underwear. I heard other voices start to laugh and snicker. It wasn't shortly I felt them on top of me taking turns with me. I was going in and out of consciousness.

After several minutes, I finally blacked out from shock. It became dark but calm and tranquil now. Any pain I had was drained from my body. I then saw my own self rise from my lying body where I hovered ten feet over the four men that were abusing me. I could see that my body was bloody and unconscious. Quentin sat in the corner counting my roll while the other three men huddled over me like dirty vultures. Immense sadness and anger started to then well up inside me as I saw this image. So much so that it was getting hard to stand it.

Then, suddenly a hand reached out and grabbed my own. All that anger and emotion suddenly melted. I looked down to see my hand was in the hand of a man's hand. One that was withered from use and had scarring from an impalement in his wrist. Upon physical contact of touching my hand, I knew who it was. I instantly then felt a heavy shame come over me though. I lifted my eyes up to slowly look into his. My eyes with tears in them, were met with the kindest eyes I had ever seen. It was then as though the load of the world was taken off my shoulders by just looking into them. Then the shame, anger, and fear inside me had vanished in a flash.

"Are you...Are you him? " I asked.

He looked at me and took my other hand. "I am who you say I am. I am here to watch over you. I have watched over you this whole time," he said whispering to me.

Upon hearing that, I cried as he pulled me into his chest. His white cloak smelled of a mixture that was hard to describe. It was a combination of wood or lumber mixed with the smell of jasmine. It was intoxicating. I cried for a few minutes and he held me to do so. Shortly, after I had no more tears to shed, he pulled away from me and looked into my swollen eyes.

"Kristen, you have turned away from me, but I have always been here. Do not be like these men below us. They seek the flesh of this world and not me. By doing so they will always be thirsty. It is then that they will stay thirsty until death which can come quickly," he said to me.

I then for the first time broke away from looking at his face and looked down at my body being mangled while the men were jeering and laughing at my naked, beaten body's expense. I then looked back up to him.

"To follow like those men is to follow death. Choose me and you will choose life," he said.

I nodded slowly in total submission. I was in awe of him. He is total love. Total truth. I knew he was perfect. I didn't want to leave his side now that I was in his presence.

"Can I choose you now?" I asked. "I don't want to leave you. I want to go with you to where you are going," I said.

He then held my face in his hand. "You will be with me one day but not now.. For you have more work to do on earth in my name. Go now and tell others. I will go and finish preparing a place for you," he said to me. I began sinking and slowly falling back to my body that lay on the floor. I looked up to see him looking down on me now from above near the ceiling with a smile. I shouted and protested when this happened but before I knew it -I sat up. I was gasping for air and coughing up blood. I looked around but saw no one. It was raining still and I could hear the water hitting the roof.

Small roof leaks trickled all around me on the floor amongst the debris and trash scattered everywhere. Lightning flickered through the half boarded up windows. Quentin's candle had blown out and the room was dark once again. There was no sign of anyone. I was now alone in the abandoned house. My money was gone and they had beaten my body inside and out to a pulp. I slowly rose and limping to the front door opened it and stepped out into the downpour. There, in an abandoned neighborhood on the front porch of a condemned crack house I took my first breath of free air that I had not breathed in a very long time. I felt a weight lifted. I felt the hope that he gave me. I was lost, but now I have been found.

It was later that night and it had gotten colder for south Texas. A Northerner had blown in turning the heavy rain into sleet and ice. I was now standing in my old cul-de-sac in Gilbertson looking into my house that was lit up for Christmas Eve. I stepped to my front door and took a deep breath. I was excited, scared, nervous, and just plain curious as to how this was about to go. But then I thought of him. I thought of him who I was just with and thinking of his presence sent a calmness over my body and made me fill with a natural joy. I was thankful I had a family to come back to. I exhaled and decided not to ring the doorbell. Let's just go on in, shall we?

I stepped into the living room noticing for the first time I looked like a wreck. I was dirty, tired, and dried blood was even still crusted on my face from the attack. I am sure I smelled of all kinds of smells that weren't full of Christmas cheer either. I had walked right smack dab into the middle of the whole family opening presents. Gift wrapping lay everywhere. Ross was on the floor under the tree next to his probably now girlfriend I was guessing. Mom and dad rose from the couch in unison like robots with their mouths wide open in shock. The room went silent except for Nat King Cole playing on the house speakers.

"I...I...love you. I love you guys. ...I am so sorry," I said, fumbling over my words while managing not to fully break down. Before I could get another word out my father rushed over and hugged me tight and I cratered in his arms. He held me like he used to. He held me like he did that one afternoon in the bathroom when I got hurt as a little girl. He held me like Jesus did today. We all then embraced and now the room was filled not only with wrapping paper but used tissues scattered the living room floor as well now. It was the best Christmas I ever had. Followed by the worst New Year's I ever had coming down off of drugs and heavy alcohol abuse.

My parents gave me my old room back. Mom played nurse and for the whole next week I felt as though I was on my deathbed. However, I thought of Jesus in those recovery days and what he had told me in that abandoned house which gave me strength. Two weeks later, my parents thought it best to enroll me in a program to keep up my sobriety and on a goal of some sort. I found myself a week later enrolled in a recovery program a few hours away from Gilbertson. It was there I met my roommate, Addison. She was a little younger than me but with the same background of a teen that rebelled and lost their way to drugs and alcohol. She, like me, was working on a second chance by being here.

It was the middle of the morning one day at the rehab center and I had just come back from breakfast to Addison and I's room. Her Bible laid on her bed open to somewhere in the New Testament. As of late, Addison had given her life to the Lord.

She had given her life in blind faith dedication, and I had actually seen him. At least that is what I still believe was reality now being months later since that day of the attack. I knew God to be true now but had not totally succumbed to him. I knew the Lord was real. I knew he was true. I just now needed to apply what he had instructed me that day. I believe Addison was sent to me to be that vehicle.

Addison walked into the room behind me and saw me thumbing through the Bible pages.

"Take it Kris. Read it. There are good things in that book," Addison informed me plopping on the bed.

"If you don't mind. I will get one of my own soon," I relied.

I ended up reading all through the night. The scripture spoke to me intensely as I imagined Jesus himself and his voice reading it aloud to me just as he had spoken to me that day. On Sundays, we were allowed to go off the rehab property. Addison and I would go into town and we started attending the small Bible church that was in a rundown strip mall there. It was there in that strip mall amongst a congregation of seventy-five that I gave my life officially to that man I met in the abandoned crack house. Of course, the moment Jesus appeared to me that one fateful day I believed. But now I was walking towards him just like he had instructed me to do so when we first held each other.

Chapter 24
Kristen Brooks

I finished typing my closing line for Sunday's sermon and then shut my laptop down. I took a deep breath and leaned back in my office chair. Staring at my pictures and bookshelf in front of me on my side office wall, I was impressed. I actually have read a lot of books in the past four years since flipping through my roommate Addison's Bible in her bed that one fateful morning at rehab.

Since the abandoned house, rehab, and meeting Jesus, life took a drastic turn for me finally in the right direction. I had finished rehab and immediately stayed and got active at the Bible church in the strip mall where I officially committed my life to Christ. I became active in their youth program implementing my testimony to the flock of youth God put before me. It wasn't a few months later after serving in the church's youth program that I felt the call to do missionary work overseas. It was then overseas and being extremely out of any kind of comfort zone that in the midst of giving my testimony and sharing the gospel that I then got the official calling that came over me. I remember the moment vividly. I was in a village in the northern part of Guana eating dinner in a stuffy hut with two families and sharing the gospel with them when suddenly that calmness and presence of the Lord came over me. It was the same feeling when Jesus hugged me inside that abandoned crack house at my lowest moment. I heard him whisper to me "Go and shepherd others. Build my kingdom and preach my word." That was my call and that was what he meant when he spoke to me giving those instructions in that abandoned house.

I flew back to the states a few weeks later and right away enrolled to finish my associates degree at a local Bible college not too far from Gilbertson. I then enrolled in seminary up in the Dallas area to become a pastor. I had done a complete one eighty and I found myself thankful for those hard days in my car because it gave me such great perspective that I apply now daily.

Being in God's plan, a position for a Bible pastor opened up right here in Gilbertson at the end of my seminary. I never thought speeding away frantically as fast as I could go in my little Honda Civic that summer before my college freshman year that I would ever end back here in Gilbertson. I went into the interview nervous but confident in what God had instore for me and what was best. I sat at the conference table in front of a full male elder board and I knew it would be a stretch hiring the first woman pastor ever at the church in a small conservative Texas town. However, the Lord was with me in that room. We all connected immediately and were on the same page. I held nothing back in that interview and they would know all of me and what I went through. I was hired a few weeks later.

While overseas at the time, doing missionary work, God had another surprise for me up his sleeve as well. I ran into my long-lost high school sweetheart, Danny Woods. The boy I left in my rainy driveway years ago. He was a part of the same missionary organization I joined and we bumped into each other, literally, at a training conference in Florida before I was to go serve abroad to share the gospel in the mission field. We spent that whole afternoon together after the conference. We walked on the beach and shared our lives and regrets since we last saw each other. We also shared what God had done in our lives since that last day together.

Danny and I talked about Brittany too. We finally could talk honestly about it. We both had carried guilt and shame from that night for abandoning Brittany on the curb without a ride and possibly then aiding in her disappearance. Danny had just dealt with it earlier than I did. He had become a Christian our senior as mentioned before. When he did, he told me he had given that guilt and weight from Brittany's vanishing over to the Lord. He said he knew God had a plan for everything and had just reasons for why things happen that may result in God just wanting you to turn to him. Danny helped me realize now that Brittany's disappearance and that whole situation, given how dark and sad it had been for me, had actually caused and set into motion me finding the Lord in the end. For Danny, it was a short road to Him. For me, it took a drug addiction and being raped in a crack house to find Him.

I still missed Britt. I thought about her weekly and Danny and I always had her in our prayers. Even though I had given all that guilt, shame, and sadness over to the Lord, she was still with me.

Safe to say though that after over five years apart and now adults, Danny and I didn't miss a beat. I wrote to him and called him every chance I got. He did the same while being in north Eastern Asia and I in Africa.

Shortly after that year abroad we came back to the states together and within weeks we were engaged. I still want to cry now about Danny and I's story and the Lord's grace and timing. I looked over at my desk at the two of us in a recent picture at the local county fair festivities. It almost was surreal we were now back in the same town.

Danny had taken a job at the local community college and we were set to wed in a few months.

I let out a long yawn and stood stretching my arms and whole body. I had been sitting in that office chair for the past three hours finishing my sermon for Sunday and finally felt prepared. I was teaching on suffering and why God allows his people and all people of the world to suffer or go through such terrible tribulations. Of course, his topic was near to my heart and something I always struggled with. But then over the recent years I began to realize through his word that suffering was a part of the world. It was an afterthought of cause and effect to sin. Because there was sin in the world there will always be suffering. It is crazy to think how so many can't accept that or are blind to it. Mostly blind because of sin really. It is a fine-spun web of irony. It was a good topic and one that I enjoyed preaching on. It is so relevant for today.

I packed my laptop into my computer briefcase while grabbing my phone. I was done for the day and heading home to my apartment. I went over to my office blinds to shut them and looked out to see our new lawn service mowing the front church yard. The service was one man actually. His name is Cal and I had run into him in our side churchyard talking to one of our church youth a few months back. He seemed innocent enough. Even though something felt familiar about him but off all at the same time. I couldn't tell you what it was though. It was like an underlying presence about him. I felt as though he was not revealing something as well. It was hard to put a finger on it. I hired him on the spot because we were in need of lawn maintenance at the time and frankly the church lawn was starting to look embarrassingly tall. He seemed to be working out nicely so far. I stared out the window at him as he pushed the mower. He seemed as though he was a lost soul. I could tell he was uneducated and probably never had left Gilbertson. Maybe even a victim to parental abandonment as a child. My heart suddenly sank for Cal as I saw him push the mower and struggle to keep the sweat out of his eyes.

I suddenly had an inspiration. I locked up my office and headed to our church kitchen that sat on the other side of our fellowship hall where we had Sunday school. Within minutes, I was making my way across the freshly cut lawn holding a sweating iced glass of lemonade I had just whipped up. As Cal saw me approaching, he cut his mower off. He avoided eye contact but smiled at me gingerly and waved hello.

"Ma'am," he said sheepishly.

"Cal, the lawn looks great. Thank you. I saw you while I was writing my message for Sunday and thought I'd bring you a glass of lemonade. I know it is hot out here today."

He took the lemonade graciously and knocked it back pretty much in one gulp. "That hit the spot. Thank ya ma'am," he said, handing me back the glass. I took the glass from him, impressed by the speed he had devoured my drink.

"So Cal you a local around here? Grow up here?" I asked. He nodded saying he has been here all his life. Studying him I again felt he had a face of familiarity. Like I had a feeling I had seen him before. Only it was an uneasy feeling and I couldn't place why that was. He didn't have a threatening presence by any means. However, looking into his eyes I could see they were hollow and flat. There was an emptiness there.

We made a little more small talk and I asked him if he goes to church somewhere. He gave me more direct attention when I asked that. I had pressed a button. He stated to me that he didn't and hadn't since he was a kid. He thought the Lord was personally a waste of time and most likely nonexistent. When he said these things, I noticed he was talking through me rather than to me. There obviously was some baggage in the God department with Cal. I challenged him and told him that was not the case and would he give me the opportunity to show him.

"I'm always open ma'am. I just know better," he said.

"Well, Cal we have our summer baptism out at the Wellings Ranch this weekend.

You should come. We would love to have you there," I said invitingly.

The church baptism was an annual early summer event where new members, family members, and or friends that wanted to commit their lives to Christ publicly could do so in the small creek that flowed through the Wellings Ranch twenty miles outside of town. The Wellings were longtime members of the church and Dave Welling was a rancher and long-time elder.

It was customary to have the whole church body cook a huge lunch BBQ and then load up every one in the late afternoon sun onto the hay trailers pulled by trucks to make the fun back road drive through the pastures to the creek. There under a perfect picturesque setting, the pastor and an elder assisting would one by one baptize the dozen members or family that were making that commitment and getting dunked. Jerry, the music director would then bust out a guitar and hymns and church songs would be sung in celebration before we all loaded back up in the trailers to go home. The church did this baptism event every year for the past couple of decades and was looked forward to.

Cal reluctantly accepted the invitation but said it would be good to get out and meet some folks. I all but agreed. Community is something everyone needs in their life whether they know it or not. Cal Sullivan said he would look forward to it. …If I only had known who or what I was really inviting to come and fellowship with us, maybe I wouldn't have been so inviting.

Chapter 25
Abaddon

Turning off of the back farm road we went over the rusted cattle guard gate. The grated metal bars shook and rattled the truck as we rolled our tires over them. It was Sunday afternoon for a hot early June day. My captive had been invited to a church congregation outing this very afternoon. I had exuberant energy building into what lay ahead. My captive, Callan, was not of the same status. He was deprived of all energy and life as I had now started to take my finishing toll on him. It would first be his body to start giving out followed by the mind that would finally crumble and cave in. I am afraid we were soon approaching the final curtain for our dear friend Callan Sullivan of Gilbertson.

We passed over another cattle guard that rattled my captive awake who had seemed to be drifting and dozing as he drove down the long dirt backroad through the various countryside pastures. I shifted suddenly in his body causing him to stir and cough profusely. I wanted him to know I was still with him and had my expectations for the day. We were scouting. Not only for our victims to feed on in my captive's basement, but for any weaknesses or souls I could penetrate in the congregation in order to turn them slowly away from The Creator they served. That was the mission as you know. The oak trees and thicket opened up suddenly to wide pastures again and we could see in the far distance a thousand yards off or so a small ranch or farm house next to a main metal barn and tractor storage barn type buildings clustered together. Cars had gathered around the buildings and I could see the assembly line of trucks hooked to pull trailers ready to haul the congregation to the baptism waters for the afternoon.

My captive pulled his old truck up along the rest of the improvised pasture parking lot and killed the engine. He finished his last drag of a cigarette and exited. We were immediately welcomed by a large heavy-set man carrying a guitar. He welcomed us and pointed to the BBQ line. Apparently, we were just in time. They had just recited the meal prayer to the Creator and were now lining up to serve.

My captive made a plate and small talk in line as church members asked him insightful questions on just who he was and if this was his first baptism outing here. Callan was never a talker. It was mostly me who had to originate conversation from within. I found it taxing but had gotten used to it. Callan simply didn't have the IQ to keep up in most circumstances. Not after I had been dwelling in him for so many years now. It was all on me in these situations. We sat down amongst the small children at the end of a long picnic table and my captive gnawed away on an over cooked beef rib. The church children around us snickered and laughed at my captives appearance and smell but it didn't bother us. We were here at the table now. Literally. We had arrived and we were hunting. We gazed around at these children wondering what could be of their futures and if they were weak and perceptible to be turned away one day. Most children are.

Cal pushed beans around his plate finishing his food and then wiped a hand of sweat away from his brow. Pastor Kristen, made her way over and greeted Cal. I remembered her. I sensed it immediately. She was the one that had approached that one day in the church yard to hire my captive's services several months back. She was the little girl I saw in the vehicle at the market that one evening on the birthday eve of the Creator. She had been one of the lucky ones. However, now coming back into our fold she may not be. Callan and her exchanged a couple of nice pleasantries and she thanked him for coming and to eat as much as he liked.

Before we knew it, the hundred-person congregation was loaded onto the back of six long hay baled trailers like cattle and we made our way down a back dirt road towards the back of the property. I was intrigued as to what was about to happen. Would the Spirit be present here today? Was the congregation capable of even drawing the full force of The Spirit or The Creator's soldiers to be a true threat to me? I was afraid of being outnumbered in this scenario and what my options would be if so.

The trailer rattled loudly as we skimmed over rocky terrain on the dirt road. There was already laughter, guitar playing, and singing that had begun. I thought I was going to be sick from the sounds of this inconvenient joy around me. Cal was prone to lose his beef ribs over it if not careful. I started to have dread build on me as we made the bend and drove down an embankment with the creek sight coming into view. If The Spirit or the Creator's soldiers were to appear here today, I wasn't going to go down without a fight but I was afraid of what I could do or be able to do.

The trucks and trailers of the church folks pulled up in a line along the bank side of the creek and the people poured out with the children and instantly hit the water for play. My captive slowly climbed out and staggered to the shoreline and sat down on the bank slipping his shoes off and putting his feet in the water. Suddenly, Mr. Guitar man, pride and all, came and stood directly over me smiling and singing about power in the blood...*Lucifer Lordship, please save me now,* I thought to myself. I couldn't stand it. Callan thought he might actually be sick but kept it down as he and I watched the congregation gather together in a tight group beside the water now. The children were called to the shore and I then saw Kristen wade out to the middle of the water. The singing stopped and it was quiet. I could breathe now.

Pastor Kristen then went on for several minutes belting promises of The Creator and of public faith. It was all such a crock...sad foolish humans. So easily influenced. What a pathetic lot. All of them.

I just needed to find Pastor Kristen's fleshly weakness and extort it. Perhaps from her past I could tempt her and then from there start the slow disease to spread throughout the congregation. That potential made days like today worth it. Anything was possible. Pastor Kristen led the congregation in prayer and that was then that I sensed it. The Spirit was fully here now amongst its people and it was strong. Rather, I knew its presence was always here but now it shined so on me that it began to burn my eyes and the scales of my skin within my captive's body. I looked up and saw two prominent soldiers of the Creator, my old kind, hovering now above Pastor Kristen as the line of new believers waded out to her to be dipped anew in the water. They were made up of shiny white drapery and their wingspan far out stretched that of mine. They were of brown and gold bronze complexion and they were staring at me as though a rat was in their kitchen. They knew I was present. They always do.

Fire and poison swelled inside. It was pure malice. I instantly leaped from my captive's body and spread my wing's lunging at the two soldiers knocking them back a hundred yards into the trees behind on the other side of the creek. Upon my vanishing of Cal's body, Cal collapsed rolling into the creek water. The baptism had stopped and so did the guitar. Church congregation members gathered around wondering if Cal needed CPR. He was weak and needed me to return to him. That much I knew.

Meanwhile, both his Creator's soldiers tossed me from tree to tree wearing me down and cutting up my skin of scales causing me to shed and bleed. I howled and hissed in the process. One soldier then pinned me to the ground by way of my wings. The other then stood over me drawing his sword of flame. If done for here, I would be exiled and cast into the lake of fire set by my Lordship. I would meet my fate now instead of later. I wasn't ready for that though. Not now. Striking like a viper, I struck my talons in the throat of the soldier pinning me down and was then able to dive under the armed soldier making my way across the creek and lunged back into my captive's body.

Cal, laying there among the group over him receiving CPR, sat up suddenly gasping for breath and spitting out creek water he had inhaled upon my exit when he had toppled over. The crowd gave him room and now with my return, my captive began to convulse in the sand. The two soldiers came upon us and drew their swords once again over the congregation before us. We had to get out of here. To stay would be death for me and ultimately for my prisoner. I was bleeding now inside from the soldiers and pure presence of The Spirit being here. My captive got to his feet and began to run. We needed to get as much distance as possible for the time being or we would indeed meet our demise. My captive and I ran through the congregation at full speed into the trees. We could make out the calls and cries of the congregation calling us back to them as we vanished.

It was nightfall now. My captive and I laid in the dirt a mile downstream. We ran for an hour straight before collapsing. Cal went into a deep sleep from pure exhaustion. I too stayed still within, licking my wounds from battle with the Creator's soldiers. I had never been outnumbered by them two to one and thought I had fought with grace and bravery given the numbers. Callan then began to stir and he sat up. His head pounded and his throat felt like the sand bank around him. The moon was out now and casted a white glow across the salt grass and trees that surrounded the slow-moving water. My captive knelt down and cupped river water into his mouth with great urgency. Upon getting his fill, he staggered to the bank again and dropped to all fours. We knelt there together for a while focusing just on his breath. Callan was struggling. His light was going out. I knew soon I would be shopping for my next home.

A strong gust of wind blew through the trees which casted a skim across the still water of the creek. I knew. I felt him and it began to burn the scales on my skin once again as I sat squirming within my captive. I started to scream in pain. Callan began convulsing and shouting for me to release him instinctively. Looking out across the other side of the creek upstream just a short way I saw him. He was slowly striding towards us. The white robe he wore against the strong light of the moon cast a shimmering glow that burnt my own eyes. It was the son of the Creator. I began to tremble. I had known of him but never yet had been in his presence on any occasion.

He stopped at the opposite edge of the creek bed and stared straight through my captive into my own eyes. He raised his arm to us slowly and pronounced, "Flee from him." With that, I was suddenly jolted and felt as though stabbed by a thousand knives. I was thrust violently from the captives' body being tossed back into the trees beyond. I let out a guttural scream and then expanded my wings that felt as though on fire while flying out over the landscape above. I found a perch on top of a large, high oak tree a thousand yards from where the son of The Creator stood. I watched out of breath as the son crossed the creek below me with pure disgust. He had made his way towards my captive and knelt beside him. Callan was mine and the son was not going to take him from me. Not on my watch.

Chapter 26
Cal Sullivan

I gasped for air as my vision was blurred. After a few seconds of gaining back my bearings, my vision came to again, and I saw that I was bent over on all fours with my hands buried in sand. My arms and chest were illuminated by moonlight. I sat up on my haunches, looking around, hearing the trickle of moving water and the evening crickets humming around me. I took a deep breath. It was the cleanest breath I had taken in a long time. I felt as though my chest no longer had a weight to it anymore, and I was thinking clearly now for the first time since I don't know when. The way I felt having possession of my own body again was a nostalgic feeling that hit me so hard I began to weep right there under the moon. Then I heard the most soothing voice I had ever heard call out to me from across the river bank.

"Callan Sullivan, rise and see me," the voice said.

I staggered to my feet and turned to the bearded man that made his way slowly across the water to me. His white robe was glowing from the moon above him. He smiled as he faced me. I knew who he was now. At least, I thought I did. He was the man I learned about as a child in Sunday school and the man Momma used to talk to me and my brother about at the breakfast table so many years ago. He took me in his arms and hugged me. I began to shed some tears again and exhaled deeply into his chest with a great feeling of natural relief. I felt the feeling again that I felt from some of my first memories as a kid being four years old again and being hugged simultaneously by my momma and poppa. I pulled away and looked into his eyes. No matter how hard I tried, I couldn't pull away from them. They had me.

"Callan, you have had evil pursue you. Evil will pursue you again but know that I am with you. Choose me, and you will be set free."

I nodded, wiping tears away. I wasn't quite sure what all that meant but all I knew was that at this moment, I wanted him near me. I didn't want to leave his side. I rubbed my eyes again to then notice he was now on the other side of the creek bed, waving back at me as he began to ascend into the air towards the moon itself. I began shouting at him to come back as I trudged out into the three-foot water after him. I shouted at him, begging him to come back, but he rose higher and higher, and I lost him in the blinding moonlight as they both then became one. It caused me to lose my footing, and I collapsed into the water, submerging myself.

Suddenly I sat up in bed. I was soaked head to toe in sweat. I got up and stood around the barren bedroom of the little white house of my folks that was lit by the early morning sun. Was it just a dream? I felt as though what I had just experienced was real. He was real...but I am here now. How did I end up in my old parents' house once again? I stepped out into the little kitchen, passing the breakfast table where Momma and I spent so many hours of my childhood and made my way to the kitchen sink. I turned the faucet on, and I drank for a long, long time, trying to quench a deep thirst that I had within me.

I shut off the faucet and then, with my huge round belly of water filled like a huge jug, I plopped down on the kitchen floor to catch my breath. Breathing was a revelation. It felt clean with no work to do so. I looked at the bare kitchen and down the hallway, confused as to why I was here. Last true memories of this place were empty night s with my uncle and guardian and the deputy's carrying me out and Momma lying dead in the bedroom there when she was killed. Now I was here as a grown and tired man. I would find out years later that I had bought this house back from the county some time ago after being condemned and neglected for years with no next of kin to grant the house to. The neighborhood took a turn for the downside over the years and commercially, nothing came to pass here and the big abandoned lot next to our house. The same one that I would stare at as a child. It was still there, standing hauntingly vacant. It was all a blur as I looked around my old and trashed house filled with literal trash, beer cans, and old TV dinners trying to gain some clarity.

What was clear is the man I had just seen in my dream by the riverside. Was it a dream? I was dumbfounded. I looked out the back window over Momma, and I's breakfast room table and saw my family's old church steeple that was lit up by the sun and poking over the top of the trees in the distance. It brought me back right then and there to the memories of God as a child. I knew the man I saw in my dreams had to be real. I plopped on my old family couch in the tiny living room and thought of Pastor Kristen and that church. I had no recollection as to how I knew her or that church, but I did just the same. Seeing that steeple lit up just now had placed that lady pastor and her church on my heart. They were all heavy on my mind now. I began to see images in my head of them from what I guessed was the past? If the past was real.

As I sat quiet in my old parents' living room all I could hear was the drone of the old AC unit working overtime to catch up with the heat of South Texas. I didn't even know what year it truly was, much less the month. The AC unit then shut off to rest and all that could be heard was the buzz of crickets outside, warning the morning that it would be a hot day. The smell of Momma's cigarettes and bacon was long gone now, and all I could smell was rotten trash that lay cluttered around me. I suddenly thought I heard the faint whimper of a woman's voice from inside the house, answered by a coughing sound. I stood up. I knew I was tired but was my mind playing tricks?

Imagining things? I pressed my ear to the wall in the short hallway next to what I didn't know at the time was the basement door to listen to the sounds. There was nothing. I didn't know I had two girls down there against their will, waiting for someone to find them. Two girls that I had put down there my own self.

I walked down the hallway toward the kitchen, still scratching my head. Metal clanging of church bells began to sound, and I walked to the breakfast table window once again and stared at the steeple out over the trees in the distance. Visions of pastor Kristen and her church and congregation standing by a waterside came pouring into my thoughts yet again. I suddenly realized it must be Sunday with church bells and all going off. I would go to church. …Or at least I would go to where I thought it was at. I wanted to know what was real. I went into my daddy's closet and found an old pair of khakis and a dress shirt covered in dirt and moth holes lying in a sack of old clothes in the corner of the floor. I gave them a dust-off and put them on. I stood in my parents' bathroom, looking into the mirror. I wiped my cowlicked hair down with my hands and some water from the bathroom faucet and then stared at myself. I barely recognized this old man from the last time I saw him as a teenager. What had happened to me? I look like a thirty-something year old that had been run over and then drowned and left out to dry too long who now looked almost sixty. I saw my father and, on that thought, I clicked the bathroom light off and made my way to the back door finding my old truck parked out back. Must be mine, I said to myself. Looks about right from the sight of it. Keys were in it.

After a couple of tries, I was able to rev the engine up and drove out the gravel dirt drive across the neighboring abandoned lot. I was off to find that church. The one I had seen standing by the river with me.

Pulling up to an open space in front of a church, I began to sweat. I wanted to blame the Texas mid-morning heat, but I knew it was the nerves. I looked up at the front doors that were open to the sidewalk and watched as the churchgoers shuffled their way inside. A fat jolly man with a big grin welcomed each one of them. He must be a leader of some sort but not pastor Kristen. Images then of the man holding a guitar singing by a river popped into my head, and I knew I had seen him before. He belonged here. Moments later, I saw her and knew it was indeed her. Pastor Kristen, in her Sunday finest and carrying her Bible, came out to also greet. I suddenly breathed a sigh of relief and knew that I wasn't crazy. I had known her or seen her before. I knew that I also had some inner desire to go and talk to her.

It looked like I would get my chance. After it seemed like most of the churchgoers had made their way inside, she looked up and saw me sitting in my truck, sweating it out. She gave a big wave like she knew me and made her way over to my truck to greet me.

"Cal! Hello sir and good morning. What happened yesterday?" she asked me.

I looked at her dumbfounded a bit. I had no recollection.

"I...I...I'm sorry, Ma'am. I don't know what you mean. We've met then before, right?" I asked. She met my face with an equal look of confusion.

"Cal, you came to our baptism yesterday. You were there sitting on the bank as we began our ceremonies and then started screaming and ran off into the woods. Are you doing okay?" Pastor Kristen then asked.

I began to sweat more as I then felt totally lost. What was I doing here? Why was I led here? Who are these people and what in God's earth is this woman talking about now?

"...Ma'am...I don't recall being anywhere yesterday. I couldn't tell you. I am lost at the moment myself," I said with a smile, trying to appease.

Pastor Kristen looked at me for a long cool moment studying me, trying to read my insides. She had a look of concern and curiosity all in one.

"Well, Cal, we looked for you half the night. I know the sheriff's department sent a few deputies as well to the property. Rancher Wellings said he spotted you lying passed out by the creek this morning. He then went to go get the medics and authorities to come to you, but you had already gotten in your truck and peeled away. He then called the church to say that he had spotted you. We sent deputies over to your house just a little while ago, but you must have missed them coming here," pastor Kristen said, informing me.

"Yes, Ma'am, they must have," I said with confusion.

"Well, I am glad you are safe now. Are you feeling okay?" Kristen asked.

"I guess I am fine. I woke up this morning with something telling me to come here. ...So I am here now," I said.

"You came to the right place. Come on in. We are packed today, but Hubert here will help get you a spot in a pew in the back. Come worship with us," pastor Kristen said, inviting me in.

And with that, the jolly man that I had seen in a vision with the guitar grabbed my hand and shook it tight, then shuffled me inside.

We stepped into a packed church that was already halfway into an old hymn rendition of "Bringing in the sheaves." People were belting the verses, both young and old. On key and very off-key alike. I made my way to the side of the sanctuary and was shown to the back row pew. I scooted in next to an older couple that met me with smiles. A few minutes later, everyone was seated and pastor Kristen took the pulpit.

She had a great presence about her and spoke to us with authority yet kindness. The sermon was on choosing God and not yourself and all the good and bad that comes with that. I guess I never really thought I had a choice. I guess as a kid, God was always there in some sort of way or another. But really in thinking on it, God had always stayed in the back row throughout my life growing up. Poppa always made sure of it that way.

Probably halfway through pastor Kristen's sermon, I began to feel that something wasn't right. I got that weight on my chest again and began feeling light-headed. The back of my neck stung and felt like it was on fire. It struck me as an all too familiar feeling. I tried my best not to squirm in the

135

pew next to the old folks. The old lady next to me leaned over and asked me if I was alright. I told her I was fine as I wiped huge beads of sweat from my face. It was then that I looked over to my direct left-hand side and saw out the huge colorful stained-glass window, a huge black figure staring at me. It then slowly morphed through the wall to reveal a huge black, and gray reptile-like dragon beast that stood over ten feet tall. His eyes glowed a light red as he stared down straight through me. I could smell his breath of sulfur and peppered smoke breathing down on me. I was locked in fear. I couldn't move or even now directly look up at the beast. I wanted to scream but my mouth was now frozen shut. I had no recollection that now pastor Kristen had finished her sermon, and the congregation had prayed and were now all standing in unison singing the closing hymn of the service. As everyone stood, I sat locked in fear with my head down on my knees. I could barely breathe from the presence of this beast. It now had fully come through the wall and landed its sharp talons directly on the back of the pew behind me, hissing and snarling at me. I was soaked now in sweat and locked in a trance by this dark thing above me.

I suddenly was then jolted free by the old woman who reached and grabbed me to rise next to her. Her touch scarred me, and I let out a loud scream that hushed the church members around me. The congregation grew silent, and stood frozen, staring at me. I rose quickly and ran screaming towards the back doors towards my truck. I could feel the whooshing of air behind me from the dark creatures' massive black wings as they stalked me from behind, following me outside. Half the church body had come rushing out as well led by pastor Kristen to see what was the matter.. I got into my truck, slamming the door shut. Suddenly, I looked up over my dash to see the large legs and sharp talons of the beast come crashing down on my hood. I gasped and then let out another scream. Before I could put my truck in reverse to pull out, the beast flared out his wings and cocked his head at me like a viper about to strike its prey. The beast lunged at me, soaring through the windshield and diving deep inside my chest, condensing itself. I cringed and leaned over the wheel trying to breath feeling as though I was having a heart attack. A hand then reached through my rolled-down driver's side window and lightly grasped my forearm. I looked up, wincing in pain, catching pastor Kristen's eyes looking down on me.

Chapter 27
Kristen Brooks

"Amen," I uttered to the congregation as we all slowly lifted our heads ceremoniously like we always have many times before. I had just completed the day's sermon and closing prayer. Cal, our lawn serviceman for the church grounds, had shown up right before the service in a very strange state but had taken me up on the offer when I invited him in for church service. He had made it out to our annual baptism yesterday and then made a rather strange exit which alarmed a lot of those who were present. I was glad just to see him show back up in one piece, to be honest. I looked over at him now in the back row corner with his head folded in his lap. I hoped that he was okay. I hoped he was just praying. I was hoping he had found right with the Lord during my message this morning, and he was now taking the proper time to make amends with Him, The Almighty, in his house. Something told me that might not be the case, though, as I stepped out of the pulpit to have Glen, our music director, bring us home with a closing hymn which was the ritual.

I made my way towards the back of the sanctuary hall to pray the final doxology prayer after the closing hymn and noticed Cal was still bent over and in what looked like some heavy pain. I took my place towards the back doors as the hymn ended. I then noticed sweet old Mrs. Phillips, who sat next to Cal during the service, reached over to aid him. Upon being touched, Cal let out a terrific scream and ran right past me, shouting and then exited the back of the church. I and the rest of the congregation quickly filed out in pure confusion and concern over what we had just witnessed. I made my way to his truck to find Cal was rocking back and forth, sitting in his own truck cab, convulsing and talking to himself. He was covered in sweat. I approached slowly and reached through the rolled-down window placing my hand slowly on his forearm. Upon feeling my touch, he snapped his arm away from me, letting out a guttural low temporal growl that could only be labeled as unworldly. He stared up at me through pure bloodshot eyes. His breathing was beast-like, and his lower jaw was crooked and seemed as though dislocated. By the sight of him, I was frightened. Where was the Cal I met out here only an hour ago?

"Cal...is there somewhere I can take you? Are you okay? You are not looking okay, I have to admit," I said, trying to keep the confidence given his state.

Cal slowly looked up at me, nodding his head in agreement profusely.

"I'm fine. I just need to get on home," Cal said assuredly. I then leaned down eye level to him and spoke softly as the gathering audience of church members on the sidewalk before we were straining to get any bits of our conversation that they could.

"Now, Cal, if you are not fine, which I don't think that you are, I want you to know I am here to help you. Anything is possible through Jesus, and knowing the Lord is in control. I believe there is a reason you are here today, my friend," I said, assuredly.

With that, Cal took a long cool beat and began pulsating as he turned to speak to me. His veins grew out of his neck, and his eyes got even a darker red.

"Your Jesus is Lord of nothing. ...You think you have control, but you do not...I am in control of this body," Cal said to me with his voice sounding as though he were a beast reptile that had crossed with a lion. It was quite disturbing.

I took a step back when hearing these sounds that were not man-like. Cal then quickly put his truck in reverse and sped out into the street, peeling away from us. I was left standing in the street, confused but also dumbfounded, while church members crowded around me.

I came to and gained consciousness. I was in the abandoned crack house again that Quentin had led me to bloody and bruised. I was alone and completely naked. I rose to my feet and looked up to see Jesus yet again standing in the front doorway in his shining white robe. He had not left me alone in this place after all. He smiled, waving me to come by his side. I walked towards him to see that he had turned and headed outside. I followed him, still bearing all to the world, and stepped outside. Jesus was now down the street, waving me forward to follow him. As I tried to catch up to him, he just got farther away from me. I began running to him to gain ground, but it was no use. I began to cry as he slowly disappeared from my view. I walked along the road alone for a bit until I came to an abandoned lot. I looked up to notice a little white house in the back of it. That is when I saw Jesus again. He was standing on the back porch steps of the little house, waving me forward. I sprinted towards him across the lot, giggling my tears away and wiping my nose as I sprinted towards him. As I reached the back door of the little house, Jesus welcomed me there and gave me a robe to wear. We held each other for a few minutes before he pulled away from me, looked into my eyes, and gestured his hand to the back door.

"Go to this place. For here in this house is where your brothers and sisters lay. If you find them, they will find me," Jesus said.

And with that, he was gone. I looked around suddenly, but there was no trace of him. He had vanished. I stood there at the back door, then staring at the door knob. I reached down to turn it and...

I sat up in bed wide-eyed. I was then hit with the rapid realization that it had been just a dream. One of many I had had about Cal over the past couple of months.

However, something had clicked. It had been months now, and I still couldn't get over what Cal had said to me and just how bizarre my encounter at the church that fateful Sunday truly was. I tried to justify his actions to mental illness and perhaps a drug history. However, just the pure evilness of what I felt when he spoke and the sound of his voice had me leaning only towards one extraordinary explanation.

I clicked on my living room light and sat at my breakfast table, pulling my laptop out. Coffee would be ready in five minutes; I told myself as I pressed the button to my coffee maker. I went to my google search bar at the top of my screen and typed in: "demon possession." For the next three hours, I got lost in the mythology of secular and biblical teaching testimonies on the topic. Some reading was just a review from what I took away from seminary and Bible college, but other information I found insightful. I studied at length about exorcisms and their realistic effects of actually working.

Hollywood had always glamorized the event of it, but I managed to eventually theorize anything was possible with God and the Holy Spirit present. There had indeed been real accounts.

Over the past several months since Cal's exit after that church service, I had been by to reach him at his residence, but no such luck. Sometimes his truck was there, and sometimes it wasn't. I knew he was there but would never come out to see me. I had then tried to forget about Cal and go about my business but couldn't let him go. He stayed with me, and I couldn't help knowing that he more than likely possessed something dark within him capable of who knows what. It didn't sit well with me. I felt the Holy Spirit wouldn't let it. Now it was clear. The house in my dream tonight I had seen before. It was Cal's house. I knew I had to find him and see what was inside. I had to see what was inside him. I knew the Lord wanted me to see inside his house where I saw Jesus. I knew I had to set Cal free.

Chapter 28
Abaddon

I sat in my captive's body, feeling restless. Cal laid on his dilapidated couch, staring up at his ceiling fan that twirled in slow motion. The TV hummed in the background but my captive was too warped to ever pay attention to the screen. It is now winter and also my most loved and yet hated time of year. 'Tis the season of the Creator's son's birth when all were merry but yet all were also distracted and depressed. It usually was a busy season for our kind, actually. Many souls were vulnerable this time of year.

It had been five months since I had been cast out from The Son's presents at the church baptism and then had to violently take back my captive's soul as ownership.

Since then, my captive was on his last leg with me. My violent return to his body after the baptism had greatly decimated any energy that he had left. Cal had not worked in months, much less moved from his bed or couch in weeks. Our hunting conquests for more souls together and come to a screeching halt as well. His face and body were frail and gaunt. More than they ever had been. He had lost over thirty pounds in the past few months. His skin was a permanent pale white now and his veins had turned black. His eyes were lifeless, showing a vast plain of nothing now. You couldn't even find my evil in them anymore. I had already begun my process of looking for a new home. At night or in the early hours of each day, when my captive was in a deep sleep, I would leave his body to hunt for my next home. There were a few potentials, but I wanted to make a grand exit with Cal before I left, as was the norm for my ego. Leave in total destruction, I say. I would have to move soon, though as I felt Cal would not be here on this earth for much more than a few weeks, I sensed.

There was a sudden stern and hardy knock at the front door that jolted my captive's eyes open to alert. Cal slowly sat up, looking around in a weakened daze. He inched his way off the couch, and we shuffled over past the living room and through piles of trash on the front door. I already had a sneaking suspicion as to whom it was. Cal fingered the ratted curtains to the side, peaking out at the middle-aged blonde woman standing on the front porch. It was that blasted pastor woman again. Pastor Kristen Brooks had come every few days for the past several weeks calling on my captive and his well-being. My captive is doing fine, pastor. Thank you very much. With any luck, Cal would be dead in day's time at the rate that I consumed him now. However, since the sighting of The Son at the river that one blasted moonlit night, I have felt a charge of conflict in my captive now that I never had before. It was that struggle that sped up this sudden wilt of his body. No doubt the damned pastor woman carried The Spirit inside her. I knew she did because my scales and wings burned just with her presence outside my captive's door. But I also felt a raw magnetism coming from within my captive, and it took great effort by me every time this woman stood on our porch and rang the doorbell. After a few minutes, the pastor woman left, and my captive and I hobbled back over to the couch and collapsed from the effort. I have to say this was all getting rather boring. My captive was getting to the point of a hermit and I needed to stretch my wings to a new perch. The hour of departure indeed was coming.

A few hours had passed, and Cal, my weak little captive, was sleeping soundly in a black sleep brought to you in part by myself, thank you. Perfect. I would now exit his body and go hunting myself for a future home. The soul market was in great standing currently in Gilbertson and the surrounding counties and I just needed to find the perfect one.

Chapter 29
Brittany Johnson

I pushed my bowl away and bent over, cradling my stomach. It had been only once or twice in the past few weeks that my captor had made his way down to see us replenish our food bowls and take out our chamber pots. I felt my stomach literally eating itself. It was an awkward and terrible feeling at the same time. The only balance to my misery was that our own bathroom stench sitting in our waste pots had built up so much that the stench was almost blinding. That helped to balance the hunger. These past few months, physical food has almost gone away, and I was now relying on spiritual food from the scripture that I read from the family Bible I had found in the dirt so many years ago. I was reading this scripture daily now:

John 16:20

Very truly I tell you, you will weep and mourn while the world rejoices. You will grieve, but your grief will turn to joy.

John 16:33

I have told you these things so that in me you may have peace. In this world, you will have trouble. But take heart! I have overcome the world.

Romans 15:13

May the God of hope fill you with all joy and peace as you trust in him, so that you may overflow with hope by the power of the Holy Spirit.

My body got weaker and weaker, but my spirit became stronger. I was beginning to make peace with myself that I would leave this dungeon finally to see my Lord's face again soon.

Ericka had all but melted away. She was frail and too weak to move really. It took me daily to convince her to take down some of the stale food and dirty water that were in our feeding bowls. She too, was starting to develop a cough that was morphing into pneumonia and I knew if things didn't change drastically soon, then she would end up like Sam. That thought haunted me. To lose her and then being in the stench down here by myself. However, I would pray, and a sudden calmness came over. I knew, however, I would never be alone ever again.

Something has changed now in my captor these past few months too. There was a darkness in this house now that I had never felt before in all the past years. When our captor did show his face, he smelled of death. He was just a walking zombie to us. He had given up sexual relations with us of any kind months ago. We were lucky when he did come down just to feed us now and or change out our pots. It had been a few weeks now until we had seen him, and I was afraid he had passed away. All the evil he had inside him had finally rotted him out I figured. Even if he was indeed dead and physically rotting upstairs, the stench was so vile down here we would never smell his rotting body above us.

There was also a presence that would come in the night now to visit Ericka and I. It was a dark one. It was one that was way more startling and primal of fear than Cal ever had within him. It was a lot more raw. I could feel it slide down the stairs like a drafty poison at night and taunt us through our cages. I could swear a few times it would whisper my name with its taunts. Then, just as quickly as it came, it was gone. Reading scripture, I had a perfect idea of what it was. And in this place, I knew that darkness felt at ease here. I just didn't know how much longer I could live in it.

Chapter 30
Cal Sullivan

I leaned over my couch coming out of a coma and vomited. My sudden sickness was then followed by a coughing spell. My lungs were on fire but at the same time, I felt relieved that I could breathe. True breaths. That weight was off my chest again, and the fogginess in my head was clear. I sat up on my couch then and looked around. It must have been in the middle of the night. The winter wind blew outside against my folks old house rattling the screen doors. I stood and walked down my short hallway towards my momma's breakfast table window and peered out. By God, it's Christmas, and I didn't realize it. I really didn't recall what season it was or how I had ended up on my couch. I could see out the window through the grove of trees in the back past the abandoned lot, the shimmering and twinkle of house Christmas lights from my neighbors. My whole house smelled foul of trash that lay in heaps around me everywhere. I walked to the kitchen sink and drank my fill of water, and then waddled back over to the breakfast table to the back window. Rubbing the cobwebs out of my eyes, I looked back out the window to see our old, tried and true family church steeple lit up and shimmering over the tops of the trees in the distance. The memories flooded in, and I looked over to see the empty chair where my momma sat at the breakfast table. A water well of emotion churned in me, and I broke down. I was lost. I was a shell of a man, and for even a worse feeling, I didn't know why. I didn't know who I was in my own house. However, looking at that church steeple peeking over all lit up in the distance, I knew I wanted out of here. Memories of Pastor Kristen and her church filled my mind and soul once again. I then envisioned the moonlit night by the baptism creek where I saw and met Him. I wanted to meet him again.

Before I knew it, I was sitting in my truck and was peeling out down the long dirt road skipping over the abandoned lot next to my little white house heading towards the street. I was going to use my compass, being that church steeple all lit up, and find some safety. I didn't need to be in that house anymore that I knew.

Chapter 31
Abaddon

I rather have to admit it felt good to expand my wings in the open night air as I sailed through the clouds that looked over the sleepy town of Gilbertson. Sleepy now, yes, but the community was buzzing with high potential prospects for the taking. I had a handful tonight I wanted to check on. I was checking status to see about a new home for me when our beloved Cal would pass on from this life to the eternal down below, but also souls I could report back to the hierarchy of his Lordship to deploy my fellow soldiers to the area. For now, we only had eight of us in the general three county area, and the demand was starting to exceed our numbers, fortunately.

With a hard stroke of my wings, I flew down below the cloud line to survey Gilbertson, who was still asleep in their beds. All that really shined besides movement on the main highway was the small twinkle of lights among the houses in celebration of The Creator's son's birth. It was a revolting sight of helplessness if you ask me. All this decor and hubbub of celebration for a bastard child born in a pigsty...I felt embarrassed for The Creator's human race. I really did.

I happen to look down amongst the neighborhood on the east end to see one solo vehicle traveling on its own. That's funny because it was not common to see one traveling amongst the neighborhoods at this time of night. Very rare, and yet, the movement and lights of the vehicle had a familiar look to it that I could not avert my gaze from. As I descended and got closer, I recognized immediately. It was the truck vehicle of my captive. What was that maggot doing traveling at this hour? How did he even have the strength at this point to be so deceptive? This will not stand.

Cruising like a missile, I plunged down at my max speed and came crashing down on Cal's truck roof with such force it physically rattled the truck causing Cal to swerve into the other lane soaring off the road. My captive's truck plunged then off the road, taking out a farmer's fence and rolled to a stop in the middle of a pasture just half a mile off the edge of town.

My captive quickly scrambled out of his vehicle as though he knew of my presence now and began sprinting and falling as he went across the pasture away from me. I hissed in anger at my frustration and with one giant leap I lunged off of his truck roof fifty yards or so and came crashing down on Cal's shoulders causing him to collapse to the ground. He let out a scream and began to squirm, but I had him locked up and trapped right within my wings. I rolled him over to face me once again and dug my sharp talons into his chest. Callan screamed in pain, which brought me delight. How dare he run off like a thief in the night to seek The Creator, no doubt, and forget all about his precious captor. His owner. I leaned in close to his face and breathed sulfur and heat from within me onto his face as I whispered his name. Callan began to scream again and resist more, but he was trapped.

"Please...whatever you are...just leave me alone. Kill me...don't care...just...leave me be," my captive pleaded in tears.

Pathetic, I'll say, but I am going to give Callan Sullivan exactly what he is begging for. I will leave him alone indeed. It is rather a time to move on. This captive has served his purpose. However, I can't leave without a tidy but grand exit. An exit that is being called for here. I quickly rose and then plunged myself back into my captive's chest, entering him once again to settle for the final climax.

Minutes later, we were back on the road together down the dark farm road back towards Gilbertson. Callan had fully submitted to me now. He had no choice. He no longer had enough strength to not do so. Ever since the river baptism, the Spirit had been chasing...and that blasted woman pastor. Callan was a robot now. With iced-over eyes, my captive drove and pulled over at the gas station a few blocks down from his dwelling. We quickly unloaded the four or five lawn service gallon gas jugs from his truck bed and began filling them. Cal then lit a cigarette and got back in his cab. It was time to end things. To move on.

Chapter 32
Brittany Johnson

"Ericka, drink some water, baby girl," I ordered her. She was having another coughing fit. I was afraid that her symptoms had turned to full-blown pneumonia now. Ericka slurped down some water like a dog and then began eating. At least, she was eating again somewhat to give her energy. However, I knew time was not on our side. She probably only had another week or so before she would risk having her lungs become completely clogged with fluid and pass away. It was the same fate that we saw Sam slip away into next to us, and I didn't want to face that again. I had, for the past few days, feasibly trying to find a way to get out of this cage I was in. I guess I never had really thought about it before. Realistically that is. I always guess deep down, I thought someone would come down here and save us, but it never came. Plus, our captor had not been down here in three weeks' time so I was convinced now he was indeed dead by the look of him that past few times he had come down here to tend to us.

I had started trying to unfasten the wiring from the back of my cage but what seemed like it would be simple really wasn't. I could only work on it for so long without passing out from exhaustion and any work I did to free myself; I found my hands were cut to shreds and bleeding profusely leaving me even more weak. I had to keep working, I told myself or it could mean very well that we would both die down here.

It was late evening on this cold winter day. The sunlight cracks through the blocked windows would soon be appearing, I felt. The basement grew cold to where I could see breath waver in and out of my body with every breath that I took when it was nighttime. The nighttime and increasing cold air did havoc on Ericka's pneumonia, and she would start her coughing spells that would last on and off throughout the night until she would pass out from exhaustion, only to wake up later the next afternoon to start all over again. I was roused awake by our captor above, who sped up to the house quickly in his truck and killed the engine. I sat up and saw, for the time being, Ericka was fast asleep. The truck door slammed and within seconds, I could hear the back door burst open. Well, I'll be…he was alive after all. It had to be him. It was no doubt his truck engine, I heard.

Like a rat, I could hear my captor scramble about and pace in and out of the house. He then began shuffling all through the house above me going through what sounded like in and out of each room. What was he doing? This was not normal for him. These days whenever he did come home, it would be straight to flop down on the couch, most likely in the living room above us.

Suddenly the basement door at the top of the stairs popped open. Ericka sat up now, beginning to cough. We both looked up and squinted to see our captor's silhouette standing dominant at the top of the stairs. He was holding something, but I couldn't make it out. It was a jug or bucket or something. But then I smelled it. Gas. He stumbled down the stairs as if drunk, waving the gas can every wear around him as he descended down. Gas trickled everywhere. He made his way over to Ericka first and without a beat soaked her with gas by pouring it all over her forehead. She let out a muffled scream as she tried to shield gas from her eyes. Her coughing started up, and she was having even more trouble breathing. Before I knew it, he had made his way over to me and dumped the rest of the gas jug all over me. The gas burned my eyes, and I too backed away to the back of my cage to create space between me and the madman. He began to roar like a beast laughing and walked back up the flight of stairs halfway before stopping. He took a beat with his back to us. I then heard the worst sound. It was the stroke of a match. He then slowly turned back to us with his dead black eyes illuminated by the small flame. He lowered his head gurgling and laughing while looking at the flame.

"Odie hanc flammam in barathrum inferni cum dominio meo coniunges," he uttered to us slowly in a voice that was not a man. I know that for certain.

I began to cry. The gasoline-only made me cry more. Internally I cried out to God. It can't be like this. He said he would save me. Jesus held me in paradise and said I would be saved. Where is he? Where is…KNOCK KNOCK KNOCK. There was a loud banging at the front door. Our captive, thrown off guard, quickly put the flame out with his fingers and uttered a deep low growl to himself as he made his way upstairs to see who would be visiting at this time of night.

After he was gone, I wiped myself down best that I could with my rags for clothes trying to get as much of the gas as possible off of me. Ericka was still having a coughing fit across from me as she moaned and cried as well in the process. I reassured her we were okay right now and to drink some of her water. Ericka began to do so but spat it out quickly. Gasoline had found her water bowl as well. I began to pray as I sat there in silence, listening to Ericka suffer lying next to me. I prayed for God to come. I prayed for him to come now as I didn't know how much more we could take now. Suddenly I heard thrashing about coming from upstairs. I heard our captor screaming all sorts of sounds that were animal-like and just straight haunting. I heard the commands of a woman's voice too but was confused as to what was going on. There would then be long gaps of silence that would then give way to more crashing sounds and loud screams. Suddenly out of nowhere came a large booming sound like a cannon had gone off above us. It was so loud and forceful that seemed to lift the house off the ground several inches and then came to rest again. The sudden house movement knocked dust down on top of our cages while kicking a few wooden foundation beams down from the floor rafters above us slamming into our cages. Wiping the dirt from my eyes, Ericka and I both sat wide-eyed, looking at each other as to what had just happened.

Chapter 33
Kristen Brooks

I clicked on the light to my apartment bathroom and splashed water on my face. I was still living alone without Danny, my fiancé, that I was to marry in the spring. He was living on the other side of town by the junior college. I stared into the bathroom mirror at the bags under my eyes due to lack of sleep, a little bit of age, and a real hard past. It was 3:30 am and I had had another bad dream of the hard past. It usually was another nightmare dealing with my attack in the abandoned crack house I was left for dead at, but lately, it had morphed to the little house where Cal lived in town. I had for the past few months, kept dreaming the same dream of Jesus leading me there in some form or fashion. It kept gnawing at me that I had to be there and go inside. For weeks, I had gone to Cal's house to stir him up and just see that he was doing okay, but I never got an answer at the door.

I flicked off the bathroom light and made my way into my living room and turned on those lights. It was early but I thought I would take advantage of my short-term insomnia and work on my sermon for this Sunday and get a head of the week. Looking at my side desk, I noticed I had left my laptop at my church office. No sweat, I'll just go to the office now and get an early, early jump start on the day. It's nothing coffee couldn't take care of later, I told myself.

Driving along the empty streets of Gilbertson in the wee hours brought back memories. I passed our old high school gym and memories of Brittany and I on the team came flooding in. Looking down at my car clock, it read 4:00 am. The time and place reminded me of all the times our basketball team traveled on the school bus, aka 'the yellow dog', for games. We would pull in at all hours of the night back onto our campus, coming back from a basketball tournament five counties away. Brittany's grandfather was always so sweet to come at that late hour and pick us up. My parents definitely couldn't have been bothered doing something like that. Even though exhausted, I still found myself and Brit cracking up with one another over the conversations and banter she and her grandfather would get into on those late rides home. I could tell her and her grandad were very close. I guess that was part of the guilt that set in. My immaturity and choices of leaving Brittany that late night on the curb not only indirectly led to Britt's mom ending her life, but I knew that because of me, I had stripped Brittany and her grandfather of their relationship and the closeness they once had. Overnight, that had been taken from them. In time, I had given all my guilt and baggage to the Lord, but it doesn't mean that the feelings and images don't flare up from time to time. I realized that was just part of being human.

I exited off of the loop at one edge of town and was about to turn into the neighborhood section where the church was when out of the corner of my eye, I noticed a few pastures away, headlights of an oncoming vehicle from the other farm road lose control and spin out before coming to a stop. I slowed down and pulled over to the shoulder. What was that? It definitely was an accident but to what degree? I decided to U-turn around and get on the farm road heading off in that direction to go inspect. It could be someone hurt and or a drunk driver needing to be reported, I told myself. By the time I made my way back around, I slowly passed the pasture where I saw that the pasture fence had been run through, and there, out in the middle of the high grass field I could see what looked like a small truck parked out in the middle of it. Its lights were still on, illuminating the pasture. Fence posts and barbed wire fencing had exploded all over the ground at the point of impact and the truck had laid long ruts across the field before coming to a stop. I pulled my little Camry to the side of the road and watched through my windshield mirrors as I reached around for my phone. Calling 911 would be best no matter what. This needed involvement from the police. I am just simply doing my civic duty here, I thought to myself. Suddenly through my rearview mirror, I saw a black silhouette cross the back tail lights of the truck, blaring red and stepping through the cloud of exhaust smoke. As I began to dial, I saw the truck then flare its reverse lights and back up, peeling away and then heading back towards its entry point. Within seconds, it entered the road again and came soaring past me. I hung the phone up. It was Cal's truck. I had no doubt in my mind. What was he doing at this time of night? I wanted to blame substance abuse again, but I knew in my gut that Cal was facing darker forces here. I put my car in drive and decided to follow. Sheer curiosity had now taken over.

I kicked my headlights off and eased around the tire shop that sat diagonally across the street from Hubert's old gas station and general store. The store was closed, but the pumps stayed on all night. I watched from my driver's side window as Cal staggered out of his car like a zombie and began pulling gas gallon jugs out of the back of his truck and filling them one by one under the yellow-orange tinted street light that hung above. It was now obvious that my curiosity had peaked to critical mass. Given the time of night and his activity, I knew it could only be bad. My car sat well over a hundred yards from him in the shadows, and even from this distance, I could tell by how Cal moved his body he was no longer a man but one possessed by something that wasn't.

Staying a good distance behind with my headlights still off, I followed Cal as he pulled away and headed to what looked like his old neighborhood. I eased slowly to a crawling stop and parked on the curb some distance on the opposite side of the abandoned lot and watched as Cal eased his truck around to his back porch and began unloading gas cans. He brought them inside his house one by one. I shut off the engine and took a deep breath. What was I to do? Was I going to go through with this? Do I just call the cops? But what do I have to go on? Sorry officer, there is a man that lives at his house here that is in possession of gas? Yes, the time of day and what he was doing add up to some suspicious activity but was it enough for the cop to act on? Plus, the underlying reason I knew in my bones and what I knew The Spirit had been telling me all this time was Cal had darkness. Police showing up would only delay an inevitable. I was being told to go into that house and extract it. A demon?...Maybe it was. It wouldn't be the police to deal with something like that, though. I knew the Lord was telling it to be me. I took a huge swig of my water bottle from my console and grabbed my Bible from the passenger seat. It was time to see up close and personal what God wanted me to go in that house and see.

I stepped onto the old creaky and dilapidated front porch steps that I had done so many times already these past few months and wrapped on the door clutching my Bible. Something told me now that I would have a different outcome this evening than all the other times I had knocked on Cal's door. I waited for a few minutes, but no response.

Maybe it was time to try the back door, I thought. Some lights were on and I just saw him literally walk through the back door. In my dreams, Jesus was even leading me through that back door. I made my way around and stepped up to the back porch approaching the door and knocked a stout knock on it as well. Upon doing so, a gust of wind also blew, causing the back door to slowly creep open halfway. Maybe that was the Lord saying, "Yes, please come in?"

I poked my head in, calling for Cal but no answer. The smell of pure gasoline hit me like a wave causing me to almost take a step back. It was dark and musty inside with only the overhead dim kitchen light on above me that flickered. Trash literally laid scattered everywhere as several mice scampered across the floor in front of me. I could see the dripping and pooling of fresh gas that covered and soaked the walls and floor around me. Directly to my left was what looked like the master bedroom, and I found myself closing the door behind me and wandering into the bedroom. More piles of trash lay everywhere, and all that was made up of the bed was just a mattress itself that lay on the floor. The place almost looked abandoned and reminders of the old abandoned crack house that I was accosted at came flooding back into my mind causing the hairs to stand on the back of my neck. I quickly exited the bedroom back into the kitchen and upon doing so, turned to my left and let out a small shriek of surprise. There standing in the hallway by the front door, was Cal emersed in the darkness. I could barely make out the shadow of his body, but his eyes had a glow of almost light red that illuminated back at me. I took a step backward.

"Cal?" I asked, swallowing hard. "Is that you?"

Seconds later, my shadowed adversary emerged into the pool of light. Cal was ragged and clutching a gas can. His face was gaunt, his skin was yellowish white, and his jaw was somewhat disjointed. Through hallowed red eyes, he growled in a low tone as he approached me.

"Sit," he said in a guttural deep beast-like voice.

I slowly took a seat at the little breakfast table. He dropped the gas can, spilling the rest on the floor, not caring. I watched as the gas gathered into a huge collective pool in the center of the kitchen. Cal suddenly struck a match out of nowhere and very robotically lit a cigarette in front of my face. The hair stood on the back of my neck, and my palms were drenching my Bible that I held onto for fear of my life now.

Cal leaned back in his chair and became more fluid now and relaxed. His eyes became almost reptile-like with his gaze. He exhaled a huge plume of smoke toward my face.

"What brings you here, Pastor?" He said in a low cryptic voice. His voice was again beast-like, but only this time it sounded ancient and that not of a man. I kept my eyes locked on his. I could feel The Spirit present, if not right outside that back door, giving me confidence now from within.

"I wanna know to whom I am talking to?" I asked. "We all know it is not Cal Sullivan," I said. He took another drag and then ashed his cigarette near the large drying puddle of gas that lay beside us on the floor.

He leaned in again, talking through the smoke coming out of his mouth.

"You are correct. I am the captor of said Callan Sullivan. I am the captor of his soul pastor. He is mine. He has been mine. He will always be mine. So why do you want him? The master you serve is dead. The Creator is weak. Bringing Callan to him is pointless. There is no hope for him now," he muttered and then leaned back in his chair. I was frozen stiff. I could feel death coming from his lips. It was a feeling that was not of this world. One I had never felt before. Polar opposite to the feeling of being in Jesus's presence. It was a feeling of zero hope and a haunting torcher.

"And what is your name?" I asked very timidly. He took a beat and luckily put out the cigarette right on the table.

"I am Abaddon. Servant of his Lordship from below. The true high priest…and I have more power than you would ever know, pastor," he said sharply.

Abaddon then lunged at me like a snake grabbing my throat and lifted me off the ground. My Bible dropped to the floor, and he then pinned me to the kitchen wall holding me by one arm. I was gasping for breath.

"Pastor, you made a mistake by coming here. You have come to your death," he said with an eerily calm demeanor. He began to squeeze tighter on my windpipe. His red and blackish eyes rolled back in his head as he began to speak to what I could make out as Latin very rapidly. I could feel myself starting to black out. Suddenly another gust of winter wind hit the house and busted the back door open. I knew now The Spirit was fully with me. Slowly through a crushing windpipe, I uttered the word. It was the word that had the meaning of all meanings behind it. I was barely able to squeeze it out of me with every fiber of my being.

"...Jesus," I mumbled.

With that, Abaddon dropped me to the ground and snarled, taking a few staggered steps back. I coughed and then regained a little bit of my voice.

"Jesus," I shouted. The demon snarled again and moaned. "Jesus!," I shouted even louder. I stumbled on all fours and grabbed my Bible. With shaking hands, I flipped to my bookmarking and began reading scripture. I was only a verse in before he had grabbed my leg. I screamed and with my first reaction, I took my Bible now as a literal weapon and slammed it down onto his head. Abaddon did not like that. He howled and screamed, crawling a few yards away from me. I then stood up over him and began reciting over and over again. "By the power of the Holy Spirit present and in the name of Jesus, I command you to come out of him, Abaddon! Be cast out! In the name of Jesus," I shouted loudly. I recited this many times as Abaddon started to go crazy. He yelled and kicked and screamed in revolt. He climbed on the wall like a spider sticking to it. My mouth dropped and dried up from fear mixed with amazement, but I continued on with my words. He crawled all over the walls and ceilings. I boldly followed him from room to room like an exterminator hunting out the last cockroach. Finally, he had had enough and made for his grand exit. There was a loud BOOM that lifted the house from where it lay and dropped it back down on its frame, causing me to stumble back, tripping over a chair. I was knocked unconscious. The last image I saw before fading to black was Cal's body dropping from the ceiling and plopping back down on the floor like a dead fish. Then...darkness.

My eyelids slowly lifted, and I could see the early sun rays of dawn starting to poke in through the tattered blinds hitting me in the face. All that could be heard was the chirping of birds outside. The demon must be gone, I immediately thought. I felt no presence of him or that bottomless feeling of fear I had when he was here. I slowly lifted my head to see that when the house lifted and fell again upon Abaddon's exit, it had created huge cracking and break up in the walls and small collapsing in parts of the old deteriorated roof. Many areas in the flooring around me had caved in. The early morning sun was now poking and shining through its rays, cutting the darkness like a knife all around me exposing the ugly trash and cobwebs that covered the house for what they were in all their ugliness and decay. It was a beautiful metaphor for God himself, I thought. That is exactly, what his light can do.

I sat up to see Cal lying on the floor face down in the short hallway in front of me.

I stared at him hard for a few seconds and could then see through his dirty white stained underwear t-shirt his back moving up and down. He was breathing. I slowly went to the kitchen sink to nurse the cut wound I was now sporting on my forehead. Walking over to where Cal lay, I then knelt down beside him and very cautiously rolled him over on his back. He then let out a series of violent coughs before slowly opening his eyes. He was very weak.

"P…pppastor," he mumbled to me.

"Shhh. Don't speak. You are safe now, Cal. …It is just you now," I said.

I brushed dirt and dust away from Cal's face and smiled at him. There was faint coughing coming from the door beside me. I turned slowly and listened. Someone coughed again.

"Relax for a second, Cal. I'll be right back," I told him.

I stood and slowly opened the door in the hallway next to me. There was a long row of cemented stairs leading downward. I made my way slowly down to a dirt floor and looked around. Rays of sun had found their way down here as well from the blast and broken glass from the ground-level basement windows. I squinted through the sun beams shooting all around me to see two sets of wide-open eyes in cages staring back at me. It was two girls. They were so dirty that they in fact blended in with the coloring of the dirt floor. Both began crying upon seeing me. I immediately went to each cage letting them free, and was appalled at their state and the extreme smell of gas and sewage down here. Freeing the girl to my right first she began to have a coughing fit upon helping her out. I stood there holding her as she coughed and cried into my chest for a few minutes. She was dirty to the point that I couldn't guess her age nor her nationality. She smelled absolutely horrendous, and I cried a little too as I held her. The girl let go of me, and I quickly went over to check on the other. I quickly knelt down again and helped her out and up onto her feet slowly. She wobbled a bit but then stood, and we faced each other face to face for the first time. A very tired, skinny, and extremely dirty black girl was staring back at me with trickling tears in her eyes. My mouth dropped a bit, as did hers, upon realizing, and my legs began to shake.

"Britt??" I whispered in shock.

She slowly nodded her head at me and exhaled a huge breath. I stepped forward, clenching both her forearms. I was speechless. I was trying to find the words for this moment. I was shocked. I was relieved. I was scared. I was amazingly happy all in a moment.

"I...I...It's you?!" I said, welling up the tears. She nodded to me and began to break down.

"I am so so sorry," I mumbled. Brittany took a deep breath, trying to catch it, and was wiping tears now from my face. "Kristen, baby, don't worry about any of that...I forgave you years ago...I am just glad you found me," she said. With that, the momentum overcame us, and we both embraced. We held each other for a long time and cried. We were so caught up in the momentum of the surprise reunion in fact, I didn't even notice that the other girl, whom I would find out later was indeed Ericka, had left up the stairs taking no chances and had gone for help seeking the police from a nearby neighbor's house. It was a beautiful thing holding Brittany in that dingy and practically fallen down basement. It was a God thing. HE had brought us back together, and HE used our separation from each other to then find HIM. The irony is that Brittany and I both would have to go find HIM in order to find each other once again. God is the best author I know.

Chapter 34
Abaddon

What a wretched mess! That blasted weak woman! If she hadn't had The Spirit and The Creator's angels there to show up, I would have literally torn her limb from limb in that house! I would have decimated her! I was more than fuming mad as I blasted through the roof of that pathetic little white house for the last time. Being banished, I expanded my wings that literally felt as though they were on fire. I cursed myself as I flew up into the night sky, heading for the cover of clouds. The scales of my skin were burnt badly and my head was pounding as though it were to explode. I had never come in contact with such a force from The Spirit or his Creator's soldiers who were so elite. I had never fought soldiers of light that were of that high rank before in my past either. I was lucky to say the least to have survived.

I looked over my shoulder to see down behind me; Cal's white house was completely covered up and shielded over now by the shining white wings of The Creator's soldiers that had banished me out. The moon peeking through the clouds of the southern sky made them shine with such brilliance that I wanted to scream, and scream I did. I rose up into the clouds and began heading north. …Oh well, I thought. On with the up and up! It was time to move on anyway. I had used up Callan as much as possible.

He was at death's door anyhow, I told myself. I only hope now, upon my exit, that it took what was left of him in the process. To one day go back under to his Lordship's kingdom below and see our dear Callan burning in t flames would be extraordinary. It would be a reward for the hard work put on my part. I was dedicated by all means to him. Why I even worked in that poor little house that I had just been rudely kicked out of for generations, I suddenly thought to myself. Callan's father's soul was much more inviting, I have to admit. He never fought me or was ever as perceptive to The Spirit's call the way our weak Callan was. I was glad to be rid of that weakling and his family.

I rose higher in the sky, soaring at a relaxed pace now and turned heading due west. There was a business opportunity now for me four counties away I wanted to go look in on. One of my fellow fallen soldiers was doing great work and had possessed a pastor of a local church in a small town there and had settled in quite nicely. He had put out a call a few weeks ago into the late evening sky as a signal though, needing help with the congregation and the church elders in particular. Given my current predicament now, I was just the fallen angel for the job. Hopefully, my mighty Lordship from the below would not get word of my banishment tonight until days from now and with any luck, I will report back that I have already possessed another soul with my fellow soldier in said church that I was now to embar on. By accomplishing this, hopefully, it would lessen my punishment for my overall failures with the Sullivan family. However, I was scared nonetheless. I was always scared as to what his Lordship Lucifer would do to me. His wrath held endless depths.

As I guided through the clouds in total darkness, I couldn't help but turn over in my little reptilian brain what could have been. Why did I fall at the beginning to become the demon angel I am now? Surely The Creator was a better host than mine currently? I should have stayed. I shouldn't have fallen and gone below to the darkness. It was selfishness. I knew that deep down, it was that selfishness that would make me burn one day to ash. That was my fate, but for now, I needed to stay busy.

Chapter 35
Cal Sullivan

I slowly opened my eyes to the pastor woman looking right down at me. She looked angelic. Part of the roof above her had given way, somehow shooting sunlight down on her from behind. Was this heaven, I asked myself? I was able to mumble out through my mouth, that was all dry and stiff:

"Pastor?"

Kristen placed her hand on my head wiping dust and debris away from my face, and told me to relax and just breathe. She told me to wait and then suddenly had left my side.

After a few minutes, I had gained full consciousness and sat up on my left side. I looked around and saw I was back in my room at my parent's old house again. How I had wound up here again, I didn't know. I looked around to see that the roof had caved in in spots and the floor and given way leaving gaping holes everywhere, top to bottom, exposing the outside. The entire house seemed to lean to one side throwing me off balance and I had to lay back down again to not be sick from dizziness. After a few minutes of laying and listening to the birds outside and cars passing by here and there, I sat up again to see a dirty and ragged-haired young girl maybe in her twenties staring at me from the opening of the doorway that led down to Poppa's old basement. She locked eyes with me for a cool half minute, staring me down to death as though I were her sworn enemy. A tear streamed down her face and by the look of it, I could tell she wanted to do bad things to me. She then quickly turned and began coughing up a storm as she ran through the piles of old trash barricading the front door. She managed to get it open and was gone. I sat there staring at the wide-open front door, rocking on its hinges while scratching my head as to why a scuffed-up young girl was down there in Poppa's basement.

As I got up, I braced my weight on the hallway wall next to me trying to shake off my sea legs from under me. I was so weak I felt as though I would keel over any moment. However, the air that ran through my lungs felt refreshing. Even for being in this place. I heard more voices and whimpering coming from the basement again. I steadied myself and made my way down the wall to the basement doorway and clutched onto the staircase banister leading down the stairs. One step at a time I made my descent hoping not to just tumble down the whole flight of stairs altogether. Midway down, I looked up to see below that pastor Kristen was holding another girl in her arms. The girl was just as dirty as the girl I saw take off out the front door just now. They both had collapsed on the dirt floor, holding each other and were crying. They both looked up at me upon my appearance and froze.

"You…you ladies alright? What ya'll doin' down here, pastor?" I asked.

They both just stared back up at me with long knowing looks only, I didn't seem to be in the know. In the distance, I heard sirens blaring and getting louder. I didn't know the sirens would be for me.

Sitting in the darkness was my downtime. I was able to relax and clear my head while turning over and over in my head how I got here. It had been over a year now since the trial, and I was sentenced to serve my term in Huntsville, Tx. The trial itself had made national news that stirred up quite the controversy. That fateful day when I had awoken half dead on my parents' floor and found the girls down in the basement with the pastor, I was arrested and held at county jail for over six months until my trial date.

Shockingly enough, the little black girl, Brittany, whom I had found down there in that basement hugging on the pastor like her life depended on it, didn't wanna press charges on me. Well now, once the media got wind that a little black girl didn't want to press charges and see a white man go to jail who had supposedly kept her locked in a basement for over ten years, well that got people's attention.

People from all corners came to cover the story. The other little girl, Ericka, was her name, did testify as to what I did to her as well as to the various other girls over the years she had witnessed me being down there in that basement. Where things really got shook up was when my attorney, that had been provided to me, threw some Hail Marys and let Brittany and Pastor Kristen both take the stand on my behalf stating, I was brainwashed and spoke of Satan and the supernatural that had overtaken me. Jurors didn't know how to handle all that I had to admit. I gotta say, I didn't either. That's what kept me up most nights now. I was trying to search every cranny of my brain for recollection of any of this but I was just always coming up short. All I remember was images of the pastor, my folks, and me as a child who went to a foster home. There was also that image of Jesus on the water under the moon that one night when he held me. I really believed though, that seeing him was just a dream. I really couldn't recall any of the darkness they said I did, no matter how hard I tried. In my loneliness day in and day out now, I thought of Jesus and what he said to me at that creek bed that one night. However, I reckon that if I had done all these awful things them girls said I had done, then I figured what he would really want with me. I was ashamed to reach out to him even though I had all the time in the world now to do so.

The prosecution was pushing for death penalty even though they had no solid evidence to go on that I had actually killed anyone. They never found one of the girls' bodies that had gone missing, and I had nothing to tell them or I would have. All the prosecution had was Ericka's main testimony to witnessing me take girls in and out of that basement to dispose of them over the years. The jury went into their room after the closing statements and stayed there for a week. The jury was almost on the verge of being called hung, but they came out on day six and had decided to give me 30 years without parole. It was a life sentencing at my age to be honest. Many were in an uproar over the sentencing, but most didn't know what to think. Word is that they still don't.

There was the familiar buzzing, and thundering noise that happened at 6 am the next morning and that's when all the very pleasant fluorescent lights came flicking on, blinding you, letting you know you needed to get up in your solitary confinement. I shielded my eyes from the glare as the light came invading in bouncing off the white cylinder-blocked walls of my tomb. …Another day is what I would usually tell myself. Another day to sit with my thoughts. I always looked forward to my one-hour-a-week recreation time to go outside and stare at the blue sky looming over high concrete walls. Amongst the sea of white I now live in, I never saw the sky so blue now. Has it always been this way? Surely not, I told myself. Staring up at that bright blue sky every week my mind would then wonder. I'd think about Momma and what she was doing up there in that heaven past all that blue sky. I wondered if she'd be her cheerful young self again by the time I got up there to her. If that was where I was going. I didn't know. I wasn't sure where God was going to place me at the moment. I was scared to ask him.

As the lights came on and that familiar electric humming noise of the lights began to drone on that would last all day, I sat up and leaned over putting on my slippers.

Prison house shoes, I called them. I was excited because today was different. Today I actually had a visitor. Someone was coming to see me. Me. The court had allowed it, and despite my popularity this time last year with the trial going on, nobody ever wanted to come and see me. The pastor lady, however, had come once or twice to talk about Jesus with me. That was all the visitors, though. Guess I wasn't that popular after all. The world had gone and got a new story to latch on to. Momma always said that was how the world works and to take no mind to it. I stood facing my door in silence, waiting to hear the drum of the guard door at the far end of the hallway outside my cell clang open, announcing that they were coming down to get me. I didn't know who was here today, but I was excited to break up my routine, if you get my drift. My money was on it being Pastor Kristen again but wasn't sure. Like I said, she had come to see me here a few times to give me encouragement and then assurance of past events that happened. Usually, she would write to me saying she was coming, but I hadn't gotten a letter. My curiosity wandered.

Chapter 36
Brittany Johnson

It was cold, wet, and rainy as I drove Kristen's car on I-10 heading through Houston on the way to Huntsville. I was nervous behind the wheel but insisted I wanted to make this journey alone. Kristen had insisted too. It had only been six months since I started driving. I had just started taking driver's education before I was abducted. I had to relearn what I lost in my driver's training. I had to relearn a lot of things. Mostly just how to be a functioning human being again, and that is taking time. Kristen has been with me every step of the way though, and I know that is a God thing.

It has been well over a year now since Kristen pulled me out of that basement. I remember vividly the cops surrounding the house as Kristen and I came out onto the front porch clutching each other. EMS came and immediately started attending to Kristen and I in the back of the ambulance before taking me to the hospital. I remember looking over the EMS nurse's shoulder and seeing Cal in handcuffs as they lowered him into the back of the cop car. His face had a look of confusion mixed with dread. I remember even at that moment feeling for him. I knew as well as Kristen that dark forces had been a hold of him but he was still going to have to pay the price. He looked at us with those sad eyes as the cop car pulled around us, heading to the station.

I was held at the hospital to hydrate and be monitored and nourished for three days before releasing me. They fed me well too. I found out that my pappy had died in the past year from a heart attack and to no surprise my momma had passed away from alcohol abuse three years prior. At least, I saw her though in paradise that one fateful day down in the basement and knew she was taken care of. She was with the Lord now, and I knew pappy was there too. Frying catfish, no doubt. Mama, however, was still alive and kicking and she brought me great food all my days while I was up in the hospital. I went to live with her upon my release and caught up on just being a human again. At night sometimes, I would wake up screaming thinking, I was trapped back in that dingy cage again. Mama would have to come in and hold me. We'd then pray together. Pray all night if we had to, but eventually, my anxiety would give out, and I'd slip back to sleep.

Kristen came to see me often to counsel me as well as catch up on what lives have been like the past ten years. We both had stories to tell. I immediately got involved with Kristen's church and her youth group program. Being around the high school kids helped fulfill something that I felt I had missed out on all those years being below ground. I studied and got my G.E.D., and then Danny helped me enroll in some classes at the Gilbertson junior college he taught at. I was on my way. It was time to get my life back on track the way you knew God intended. The way Jesus told me it would when I saw him while being down there. I was free. Free to help build his kingdom now.

The day I walked up out of the basement, I took that dirty old bible I had found buried beside my cage with me. I then continued to use and read it every day. After speaking with Kristen about Cal, I knew the darkness and possession that Cal had faced. That mixed with my own personal darkness being down there in that dungeon with a man that I knew was not man; I knew Satan was at play. I was able to pray with Kristen and Danny at their house, and we prayed all together one night to forgive Cal for what he had done. We all acknowledge that he was not in control. Satan and darker forces were at work in him. No matter how many times though, I kept telling myself that I was still gun shy to go see and visit Cal. Why would I go? Kristen had been a handful of times. Mostly out of curiosity, but she said God had a hand in destiny for her to meet him in order to find me. She thought he deserved salvation with the Lord just as much as the rest of us...which was none at all. Kristen said we are all sinners and have come short of the glory of God. Kristen pointed out that we are all truly unworthy of everlasting life and being in eternity with Him, but it is by his grace we are able to do so one day. By his son. Kristen told me we all are loved and made the chance to know Him. It was our duty now as Christians to go and show that same grace that He had shown us. That grace even extended to Cal, my kidnapper.

Kristen had been begging me for weeks to go and see him. Kristen had gone a handful of times to see Cal and witness to him to see if indeed he would accept Jesus, but he was always too ashamed for what he had done. He felt he didn't deserve to know Jesus further besides seeing him that one night in his dream beside the creek he told her. Kristen thought I could break that mindset he had by going and talking to him. Cal seeing my forgiveness and grace towards him would be the end all to knowing God's true love. I knew deep down that was one hundred percent true, but I said no to Kristen for months stating what I had to say wouldn't matter. Deep down, I knew it to be fear and fear alone. It was really just the fear of seeing Cal and immediately being launched back into that old basement laying half naked and weak on a dirt floor. I didn't want to go back to those memories if I could avoid it. That was what was keeping me away.

However, I knew it was the Holy Spirit at night while lying in my mama's house that kept speaking to me to go and visit Cal. I couldn't shake it. The more I prayed and read his word I knew it was so. I realized that it wasn't about me or my fear at all. I needed to get out of my own way and let the Lord do his work. Days later, I found myself on Interstate forty-five , just thirty minutes away from Huntsville prison. My palms were sweaty on the steering wheel from the nerves, but my foot stayed on that gas. It was time to face the man from the basement.

I had made my way through the prison gates and parked. I had to check in and go through security clearance for about twenty minutes, but before I knew it, I was standing in a long line amongst family members of inmates on the outside entrance ramp into the visitor's wing of the prison. It was still cold and rainy, and I had forgotten my umbrella. A loud buzzing sound at the entrance door went off, and we all shuffled in like cattle. We were ushered in by a series of guards to our designated booths. I sat down in my little square cubicle, number eight it read, under the bright fluorescent lights facing a wall of glass. My heart began pounding, and my breath got heavy. I didn't know how this was going to go, but I knew the Lord wanted me here. I said a small prayer to myself to settle my nerves as the inmates began to file in on the other side of the glass through a door towards the back of the room. The line of the inmates' orange jumpsuits burned bright against the white walls around us. Then just like that, Cal sat down in front of me with the thick glass wall dividing us.

He sat staring down at his hands. He then placed a mailing package envelope on the table in front of him. I couldn't mistake the shape and size of it. It was the package I had sent him a few months back. He hadn't opened it since it had arrived. He would not make eye contact with me. He looked better than when I last saw him. The darkness under his eyes was not as black now, and he had gained some weight. He still carried a hard past on his face and looked older beyond his years, but the color in his cheeks and face had returned. He trembled with nerves, I could tell. We both in sync at the same time, reach for our phone receivers. Cal had still not dared to look up at me.

After a long beat, I decided to break the silence in an effort to hopefully break the tension.

"Hey Cal, how you doin'," I asked.

"I didn't know it was gonna be you…thought maybe it was as gonna be the pastor lady that come to visit me again," Cal said, mumbling. His eyes remained down.

"Well, Kristen thought it best I come to see you. She said it be good for you," I stated to him.

"Oh, she did?" Cal asked curiously. "I agree with her too," I said.

I leaned in closer to the glass as if trying to catch his eyes to connect. I felt at peace now. I knew this was simply a man in front of me. A man that didn't have control of himself during those dark times. A man that really, through the long haul of it all is still having a harder time than I ever did being in that basement.

"Cal, I just wanted to come up here and say I forgive you. I know it wasn't you that really did those things to me. You weren't in control. Even if you were…I forgive you, Cal. I am not mad at you." I looked down, noticing again the mail package with my name on the return address corner of it.

"Cal, you hadn't opened up your package yet," I said.

"Yeah…. I saw it was from you and…I guess…I guess I just done afraid to open it," he said, scratching his head.

"Well, I'm here now, and I am telling you it's okay. Please open it. It is a gift for you to have," I said warmingly.

Cal then took a beat and looked up to me with a sheepish stare. I nodded to him slowly with assurance. He took another beat and then tore it open hesitantly. He slowly pulled out the old dirt-stained Bible that I had found in his basement. A bookmark of some sort was sticking up out of the top.

"I guess that's your old family Bible there, Cal. I found it in the dirt next to my cage when I was down there. Take a look at that bookmark there," I said.

He slowly thumbed to the bookmarked page and pulled the old black and white photo of him with his family as a boy from the pages. Upon seeing this, he began to cry.

"That I take it is you and your family, Cal? ...Good looking fam," I said.

"...yeah, look at that...There we all are. I'll be damned," Cal said, nodding slowly and wiping the tears from his eyes.

"Cal, I came here to thank you," I said in a low but serious tone. He looked up at me immediately.

"I want to thank you because I look at it this way....If I hadn't gone down there where I went. I don't know if I would have the relationship with the Lord that I have today. I don't know if I would know Him like I do now. That Bible as well. That Bible was my hope. It is what led me down there all those years...Being down in that hole in the dark around all that death...all I had was the Lord. I found him there. If I had never gone down there, I don't know if I truly ever would have found Him. So for that, I say thank you."

We were both crying now and rubbing tears from our eyes. The guard came and brought a tissue box for me.

"I just....I am so sorry. I did all that to you. I am just so sorry that happened..." Cal said, breaking down. I hushed him quietly to silence.

"Don't be. Don't be. Cal, I want you to have what I have. I want you to have peace. I want you to know Him like, I do. To accept Him. You have been on the opposite side of the Lord for so long. I wanna completely bring you out of the darkness," I said. Cal took a long beat, lost in thought and rubbing his eyes staring down at his family picture.

"I just know I am unworthy ma'am...after all I did..."

"You didn't do it, Cal. I know you didn't," I said. "There were dark forces in that house that I know was making you do all that you did. I knew because at the witching hour most nights, that darkness, that presence would come by itself to visit us down there. Not you. Just it alone, " I said informingly. "Plus, Cal, we are all unworthy and come short of the glory of God. Even it had been you and only you, God still loves you. He would still forgive you. You are still worthy with his son. That is why there is grace.

170

Grace in his son. His death takes it all away. It takes that guilt and shame that I know you are holding still inside there and it dissolves it away."

Upon saying that, Cal looked back up at me and locked eyes. "You just have to let Him in," I said. Cal kept his eyes on me, still wiping tears, and slowly nodded.

"Cal, will you pray with me? Will you pray with me for his acceptance?" I asked. "He loves you. I love you. …And it is the greatest love you will ever know. It is a love that is bigger than any race, demon, basement, or dungeon that could ever try to come in between it. It's the love of Jesus Christ," I said. We both sat in silence for a while, wiping the rest of our tears away and letting sink in what I had just said to him.

"Mr. Sullivan? Will you pray with me?" I asked softly. He nodded slowly back at me with a half-smile. "Good. Let us pray then…Dear Father God, we know we are sinners…"

CPSIA information can be obtained
at www.ICGtesting.com
Printed in the USA
BVHW040911060423
661869BV00009B/147